Elisa was brought up by her grandparents, Edith and Robert Clayton, who lived at 22 Lake Lock Road, Stanley. She attended St Peter's school and Stanley Modern School, and every Sunday, she accompanied her grandparents to the services at St Peter's church—and every other holy period of the year.

Elisa has travelled to various countries of the world, but her favourite country is USA.

Eric, her husband, bought a house for them at Rapid City in the Black Hills of South Dakota, and it was there that she finalised her first book.

They also started a property company and owned a number of houses in the Black Hills area.

Elisa also personally investigates, and has written books containing, various kinds of factual psychic phenomena, which include hauntings, ghost sightings, poltergeists, and UFOs.

She has also written fictional horror stories.

In her spare time, Elisa enjoys oil painting, speaking at various Women's Institutes and knitting for the charity of her choice.

I dedicate my book to my husband, Eric, and my daughter, Lesley Anne.

And my late daughter, Dawn.

Elisa Wilkinson

GOLDBERG HALL

AUSTIN MACAULEY PUBLISHERS™
LONDON • CAMBRIDGE • NEW YORK • SHARJAH

Copyright © Elisa Wilkinson 2023

The right of Elisa Wilkinson to be identified as author of this work has been asserted by the author in accordance with section 77 and 78 of the Copyright, Designs and Patents Act 1988.

All rights reserved. No part of this publication may be reproduced, stored in a retrieval system, or transmitted in any form or by any means, electronic, mechanical, photocopying, recording, or otherwise, without the prior permission of the publishers.

Any person who commits any unauthorised act in relation to this publication may be liable to criminal prosecution and civil claims for damages.

This is a work of fiction. Names, characters, businesses, places, events, locales, and incidents are either the products of the author's imagination or used in a fictitious manner. Any resemblance to actual persons, living or dead, or actual events is purely coincidental.

A CIP catalogue record for this title is available from the British Library.

ISBN 9781398477650 (Paperback)
ISBN 9781398477667 (ePub e-book)

www.austinmacauley.com

First Published 2023
Austin Macauley Publishers Ltd®
1 Canada Square
Canary Wharf
London
E14 5AA

Table of Contents

Chapter 1: Luke Hoggs, the Farmer	13
Chapter 2: Samuel Goldberg, Owner of Goldberg Hall	17
Chapter 3: Death from Suicide and Shame	25
Chapter 4: A Mother's Revenge	34
Chapter 5: The Final Resting Place	38
Chapter 6: The Aftermath	44
Chapter 7: Hilltop Grange Manor	47
Chapter 8: The Interior of the Grange	53
Chapter 9: Moving into the Grange	59
Chapter 10: Jack	65
Chapter 11: The Police Investigation	68
Chapter 12: Reminiscing	71
Chapter 13: The Accident	76
Chapter 14: The Aftermath	82
Chapter 15: Strange Happenings	86

Chapter 16: Who's There?	92
Chapter 17: Sally	96
Chapter 18: Sally Part 2	100
Chapter 19: Strange Happenings	104
Chapter 20: The Outbuildings	111
Chapter 21: The Party	116
Chapter 22: Panic	124
Chapter 23: Leave the Grange	129
Chapter 24: The Introduction	136
Chapter 25: The Unexpected Guest	142
Chapter 26: The Briefing	149
Chapter 27: Proof	155
Chapter 28: The Investigation	158
Chapter 29: The Cellar	163
Chapter 30: History of the Hall	171
Chapter 31: Mary and Susan	177
Chapter 32: The Woman in Black	181
Chapter 33: The Disappearing Corpses	185
Chapter 34: Possession	191
Chapter 35: The Homecoming	198
Chapter 36: The Arrival of Alex and the Team	202
Chapter 37: Sad Memories	205
Chapter 38: The Attic	209

Chapter 39: Death at the Grange	**221**
Chapter 40: Epilogue	**226**
Back Page	**228**

All of the characters and properties in this book are fictional.

No matter how hard you deny your lies and deceit.
You cannot escape the fate you shall meet.
In the end I will catch you
Wherever you hide.
So, beware I am waiting.
For your soul shall be mine.

—Elisa Wilkinson

Chapter 1
Luke Hoggs, the Farmer

Huge flakes of falling snow fell upon the farmer's snow-covered head and shoulders as he leant forward battling against the elements of the driving winds and icy storm as he crossed the land at Melham, North Yorkshire, with his old faithful sheepdog, Lucy.

Chunks of ice were already forming on his beard and eyebrows, but the scarf tied tightly about his head and ears managed to keep some vestige of warmth about his weather-worn face. Luke Hoggs knew where he would find his sheep. They would be huddled together alongside one of the dry stone walls. The wall was the only protection that the open moors offered against the howling winds and driving snow.

Luke had noticed earlier on in the year that there had been a significant change in the weather conditions, and not wanting to take any unnecessary risks, he had brought the sheep down to the lower pastures where he could keep an eye on them. He grimaced at the memory of when he had last seen weather as bad as this. It was several years ago when he and his dad lost a full herd of dairy cattle and lambing sheep due to the extreme weather conditions and prowling hungry wolves that were now howling and signalling to one another where they could find their next meal.

Luke was determined not to let that happen again and patted the gun he had tucked into his belt, and the razor-sharp knife he was carrying to defend himself and Lucy. This precaution he was taking for protection was not only from the wild animals but from the nomadic travellers as well.

With having to survive in these hard times and earn a living on a tied farm, Luke couldn't afford to lose his stock of eight sheep, not after the problems of theft that the cattle and sheep farmers had been having just of late. Not only that, Luke grumbled to himself as he became even angrier when thinking about the greedy land owner, Zacharia Goldberg, wanting almost every penny the poor people earned and taking whatever he wished, be it cattle, sheep, pig, fowl, crops or wheat for his elaborate banquets and feasts, without reimbursing the poor farmer.

Nevertheless, Luke and most of the farmers had managed to struggle on and make their way through the period leading up to Christmas and into the new year.

He had already herded his six cattle inside the space below his cottage and decided that rather than risk losing his sheep he would bring them in from the pasture, on an agreement with his neighbour Jamie Broadhead, he had herded them into the low space below Jamie's cottage, where they would be safe from the freezing cold temperature and predators searching for food. They would also provide warmth to the living quarters above throughout the time they would be kept there, along with Jamie's half a dozen chickens.

At the time he couldn't make his mind up which were the worst predators—human or animal.

In those days, cattle and sheep were kept in the lower space of a cottage. The heat from the animals warmed the house.

When he was assured that all of the animals and beasts were securely herded inside, Luke dropped the joist into the brackets on either side of the wooden doors and pushed the cast iron bolts into place, ensuring that neither man nor beast could get inside without him knowing. He then slowly made his way up the stairs into the warmth of his single room. The first thing he did was stoke up the fire and then took an old rag to pat Lucy's wet fur dry and poured himself a jug of ale.

As he sat in his rickety old rocking chair, in the flickering candlelight he thought of his two sons, Robert and William, who were only thirteen and fifteen years old. They had been pressganged and forcibly taken to join *The Adventurer*, a sailing ship owned by Lord Goldberg. Both Luke and his wife, Sarah, had been devastated when they learned that the ship had floundered in a storm and all hands were presumed lost at sea.

Then worse was to come when their daughter, seven-year-old Lydia, had suddenly gone missing. A search party had been quickly formed but the girl was never found. It was too much for Sarah to cope with and she died. Luke said it was from a broken heart after losing their sons, then her last surviving child. But tongues wagged and it was strongly rumoured that she had been taken for one of the gentry's orgies.

Chapter 2
Samuel Goldberg, Owner of Goldberg Hall

Lord Samuel Ezra Goldberg inherited the ancestral 300-year-old Goldberg Hall from his father, Lord Ezra Zacharia Goldberg in the late 17th century, along with the lands, surrounding villages and hamlets, plus complete control over his deceased father's assets.

The prestigious Hall stood in a vast acreage of land surrounded by trees and exotic shrubs that he had collected from his many travels throughout the world.

Italian hand-carved marble statues were situated in perfect alignment along the drive leading to the hall. Two Italian carved marble fountains stood on either side of the lawn just a few yards away from the Hall. These sent huge jets of water spurting high into the air, then fell into a basin that overflowed into the base of the fountain where colourful ornate oriental fish swam.

The perfectly manicured lawns were surrounded and bordered with flowers that blossomed giving an array of colour all year round. But all of this beauty and splendour however, was lost on its new greedy owner, Lord Samuel Goldberg.

Samuel was a six-foot tall, 45-year-old, handsome, strong-willed, muscular man who didn't give a damn what people thought about him. He was a much hated, sanctimonious, self-centred, arrogant bully who used and abused anyone to achieve his own selfish ambitions; he trampled anyone who stood in his way. Like his ancestors, he didn't pay the architects or the builders of the hall's extensions half the money they were due, nor the carpenters, artists and a multitude of poor people who had trusted him for their wages.

The more wealth he accumulated, the more arrogant, greedy and ambitious he became. He owned shipping lines, gold, silver, diamond and other precious stone mines, along with rare minerals throughout the world. He also owned coffee and cotton plantations, then as the railroads became a more popular commodity, he bought controlling shares into those.

Whatever appeared that would increase his wealth, he bought into at low prices, and sold at high, then sat back and watched as the profit soared.

His beautiful 38-year-old wife, Hannah, was a slim woman of a delicate but shapely build, with green eyes and long red hair that fell in natural curls and ringlets about her shoulders. She also had a fiery temperament that coincided with her flame-red hair. Her stature was approximately five foot two inches tall, and she hated her husband.

At 1 pm Friday afternoon, Hannah was just leaving the Hall and was travelling to visit her sister with whom she would be staying for a number of days. The main purpose of her journey however, was to convey the news of their 16-year-old daughter Elizabeth's betrothal to a fine upstanding young gentleman. To whom she was to be married the following spring.

Neither Samuel nor Hannah acknowledged one another as the carriage, drawn by two thoroughbred horses, swept past him and out through the gates. He did however breathe a sigh of relief as he watched the carriage disappear from sight and headed back into the house, where he poured himself a large glass of port then seated himself in front of the fire.

With the two Irish wolfhounds laid at his feet, he sat staring into the fire's dancing flames and cursed out loud when thinking of the problem that had unexpectedly arisen. Their daughter, Elizabeth, had to be left behind as she was feeling too ill to travel. Suffering from a bad migraine, she had confined herself to her room.

Nevertheless, with Hannah out of the way, Samuel sent word for one of the stable lads to saddle his favourite horse and bring it to the front of the hall. Within a short space of time, the butler came to inform him that the fiery, white Arab stallion, which he preferred to ride, had been brought to the door.

Samuel took his time finishing his drink and remained seated as the butler helped him into his riding boots. Then when he was ready to leave, the butler wrapped his cloak around his shoulders, while at the same time lifting Samuel's mane of thick, long black hair that was tied at the nape of his neck with a leather thong. The butler then pulled the dark green leather riding gloves over his hands and handed Samuel his hat.

Without a gesture of acknowledgement, Samuel strode outside, mounted his horse and galloped away to where he would be meeting his three associates—Jack, Victor and Fredrick—who were already half inebriated from the wine and beer they had been drinking while waiting for Samuel's arrival at the designated brothel. Samuel was greeted at the door by the Madam who took his gloves, cloak and hat, then led him up the stairs to the private room where his presence was awaited by his three associates and four women.

As soon as Samuel strode into the boudoir, with the assistance of his chosen woman, he was quickly stripped of his clothing and felt his manhood stirring when seeing the naked high-class courtesans being fondled as they straddled the three already naked men.

The men then settled down to a night of debauchery, before returning to Goldberg Hall.

It was two-thirty the following morning when the four men arrived home to the Hall, where the butler was waiting to greet them. As soon as they were through the door, Samuel ordered the weary butler to bring soft shoes for everyone and a number of bottles of wine, champagne and fine port from the cellar and something to eat.

The butler did as he was ordered, then assisted the men in removing their riding boots and placed the soft leather shoes on each man's feet, before leaving the room.

"I wish you could find me another seven-year-old like the last one I had," James slurred, glancing bleary-eyed in Samuel's direction and laughing lecherously. "She was good, she fought like an alley-cat, that's how I like them, scratching and fighting," he garbled spilling the goblet of fine wine over his clothing.

"I prefer boys of all ages," Fredrick slurred. "Here's to all their tight little arses," he slurred drunkenly raising his goblet in a mock salute.

"Well, I prefer females," Samuel said, "preferably after they've been stripped and hosed down to get the farm stink off them." His words sent raucous echoes of laughter vibrating around the vast walls.

For a time, the men were lost in their own thoughts as they bit down on cold turkey legs and ham and guzzled wine, champagne and port. The mixture of the alcoholic beverages obliterated all sense of decency and reason from their warped minds, resulting in the drunken men wanting to do something different.

That was when Samuel had an idea. "Let's go upstairs and talk to my little girl," he slurred picking up the silver candelabra and staggering towards the staircase where he misjudged the step in the darkness and collapsed into a heap, cackling with laughter. "She will be lonely without her mamma to talk to."

One by one, the men crawled giggling up the richly carpeted staircase then dragged themselves to their feet as they staggered across the landing towards Elizabeth's bedroom door.

"Shush," Samuel whispered holding a finger to his mouth to the woozy men, as he slowly turned the door handle of the room where Elizabeth lay fast asleep in her bed.

"Who's first?" James whispered.

"Me of course, I'm her father," Samuel hissed in the darkness.

Stripping off their clothing, the four men moved towards the bed where the unsuspecting girl lay. As if sensing someone in the room, Elizabeth mumbled sleepily, "Is that you, Sarah?"

But when receiving no reply, she sat bolt upright and screamed at the sight of her father and the three naked men in her bedroom.

"Papa," she screamed pulling the covers around her neck to cover her flimsy night-clothed body. "What are you doing here, and who are these people?" she cried in fear.

"Shut up," hissed one of the men clamping his hand over her mouth to stop her from crying out to summon help, while another took hold of her flailing arms and held them above her head.

The third man dragged the bedcovers from her, then tore the nightdress away from her body and grabbed hold of her ankles to spread her legs wide apart, while her father watched with a stupid grin on his face before moving forward and sliding his fingers deep inside her vagina; with his other hand, he began caressing her small but firm rounded breasts.

Terrified and knowing what was about to happen, Elizabeth struggled to release their holds, but she was no match for the four drunken men's strength. Tears streamed down her cheeks as she sobbed helplessly, and was almost sick when her own father climbed onto the bed and straddled her, then forced his huge penis into her vagina taking away her innocence with every grunting push he made.

"The first one's on me," he guffawed loudly. "We're going to keep the name Goldberg going through you, my sweet, you will have my child. Wrap her legs around me, I want this to reach its target, then I will give her something she will remember me by," he thundered, giving a deep threatening growl.

Elizabeth could smell the alcohol and cigar smoke on his breath when he pressed his lips to hers, then making guttural sounds he shuddered as he orgasmed, discharging his hot sperm into his own daughter's womb.

"No," she screamed, rolling her head from side to side. "Not my own papa! Mamma, where are you!" she screamed.

"Shut up, you stupid little bitch," her father snarled, slapping her face from side to side. "Who's next?"

James, who had been holding her legs apart, leapt on top of the poor defenceless girl and howled as he took his pleasure. "That was the best I've had since that little brat you brought me last week," he slurred, turning to face Samuel with a stupid grin on his face as he dragged himself from the bed. He then fell to the floor where he lay snoring as a drunken stupor overcame him.

"Fredrick, you're next," Samuel called to his friend.

Fredrick didn't need much persuasion; he turned Elizabeth over and entered her anally, causing the wretched girl to scream with pain as he tore into her.

Elizabeth's personal maid, Sarah, whose room was next door to Elizabeth's, had been alerted by Elizabeth's pitiful cries and had peeped through the partially open door. She almost fainted with shock at the sight of what she was witnessing.

Her hand flew to her mouth to stifle a scream, when realising the evil situation that was occurring and immediately ran downstairs and outside to the stables, to where Peter the stable boy slept and woke him begging for his help, as she explained in a quivering voice what was happening to Elizabeth.

Knowing Samuel's vicious temper, the pair crept silently up the servants' staircase until reaching the landing, then tiptoed across the carpeted balcony, reaching Elizabeth's room, and peeped around the door.

Aghast by what they were seeing, both Sarah and Peter knew that their master would have them flogged to death if he was aware of them witnessing what he was doing.

"Sarah, keep out of the way, I'm going to let her ladyship know what's going on here."

Peter bounded down the servants' staircase three at a time and raced to the stables where he took one of the fastest horses. Knowing that time was against him, Peter didn't bother to saddle up, but jumped onto the horse's back and raced in the direction of Maudlin Manor.

In the meantime, Elizabeth's father took his daughter again, only this time there was no fight left in her, she succumbed to his every whim, and was almost ill when he had knelt over her head and forced her mouth wide open to push his throbbing penis down her throat.

Chapter 3
Death from Suicide and Shame

Two hours later, Peter arrived at Maudlin Manor lathered in sweat from himself and the horse. He had pushed the mare to her limits in his effort to reach and inform his mistress of what was occurring while she was away.

At first, Hannah could not believe what she was being told, but after recovering her senses, she didn't bother packing, but ordered her coach to be brought immediately and raced back to the Hall.

"Please god," she prayed as the tears coursed down her cheeks. "Please let my daughter be safe."

But she knew deep down that her daughter was now ruined, and when her fiancé discovered what had happened, he would not wish to marry her, neither would any decent young man, come to think of it.

For a nerve-wracking three-hour journey through the night and until the early hours of dawn, Hannah strove to control the anger and emotions racing through her. The hatred against her husband was almost unbearable, but her largest concern was for the safety of Elizabeth, knowing that she would be unable to cope with the abuse that had been forced upon her.

Hannah would have no peace of mind until she had seen her daughter to comfort and help her through the degrading violation that had been forced upon her.

In the meantime, Sarah had almost collapsed when finding that Elizabeth was dead. When seeing her bloodstained arms, face and the lower part of her naked body, and noticing the vomit on her silk lace pillowcase and the stains on the silk sheets, she immediately understood the appalling circumstances that Elizabeth had been forced to endure, also the seriousness of the situation. Sarah then realised that she would be needing help in cleaning Elizabeth's body before her mother arrived home.

She had asked Maria, the downstairs maid whom she knew that she could trust to say nothing of the brutal attack, for assistance. In tears, the two women had carefully washed Elizabeth's cold, battered body. They then removed the blood and vomit-stained sheets and pillowcases from her bed and hid them downstairs in a place where no one would think of looking. The stained linen would be safely stored as evidence of the attack for the police to use when they arrived.

They next dressed Elizabeth in her favourite pink dress and shoes, brushed her hair and arranged her on the bed, making it appear as if she was sleeping.

Hannah, however, wasn't prepared for the sight when she arrived home, where she found Samuel, along with an inebriated man, lying naked, sprawled across Samuel's four poster bed; another was slouched, snoring in the deep leather winged armchair near the fireside.

Filled with disgust and in a furious rage, Hannah hurried towards Elizabeth's rooms and let out a cry of surprise and anger after tripping over another naked drunk, who lay snoring on the floor outside of Elizabeth's open bedroom door.

But one glance at Elizabeth's white, bruised face and motionless body, Hannah could see that her beautiful daughter was dead.

"Oh no," she gasped, feeling her legs giving way and she dropped to her knees beside the bed.

Then, taking hold of her daughter's cold and stiffened hand, she let out a heart-rending wail of sorrow.

"My baby, my beautiful baby," she sobbed, "what have they done to you?" she screamed.

For over an hour, Sarah watched and listened to her mistress's heart-broken, grief-stricken sobbing as she knelt beside her dead daughter, before moving forward and gently raising Hannah to her feet and helping her into a chair beside the bed.

Numb with shock, Hannah grabbed hold of Sarah's comforting hand and held on to her for the support and strength that was now depleted from her. Then after siting for a while staring at her daughter's inert body, she realised that it must have been Sarah who had neatly brushed Elizabeth's golden hair and dressed her in her favourite pink silk lace dress and matching shoes.

Sarah had placed the gold and silver cross around her neck that had been given to her many years ago by her favourite Grandmama Darwin.

However, on the bedside table was a damming note to her mother describing every despicable torment she had been forced to endure by her own father and the three men.

Yet the most heart-breaking line was the apology for taking her own life.

Hannah gave a low despairing moan as she read the damming letter and reached forward to hold her daughter's hand again. Then she noticed that the diamond and pearl ring that had been given to her on her betrothal was nowhere to be seen.

For a few tormented moments, she sat staring helplessly at her daughter's body, and through her grief she felt an intense hatred and anger boiling inside her.

"I shall make sure they hang for this," she vowed to her only beloved child. "You will have your revenge through me. Sarah," she said, turning her tearstained face towards the loyal maid, "has anyone contacted the police yet?"

"Yes ma'am, the police have already been contacted and are on their way to the Hall," Sarah replied, knowing that it was a hanging offence that had occurred.

Hannah then called for Thomas, the estate's handyman, who was a hefty six and a half foot tall, scar faced from many fights, a rugged and sturdy man, with bulging biceps. With a short stubbly whiskered face and long prematurely grey hair, he was a loyal man who could be relied on to help Hannah and Elizabeth at any time.

After regaining her composure, Hannah ordered all of the staff, most of whom were unaware off the terrible atrocity what had occurred there that night, to immediately assemble in the drawing room. She instructed them that they must only inform the police of the three drunken men's involvement regarding the rape and death of her daughter. Her husband allowing it to happen was a different matter, she would deal with that problem herself at a later date.

When the briefing was over, the servants returned to their duties knowing that if they spoke out of turn, they would lose their jobs. The mistress would not give them a reference to enable them to find future work elsewhere, therefore that would be fatal.

Hannah knew that Thomas was a completely loyal man who was devoted to herself and to Elizabeth, and she offered to pay him handsomely if he helped her get rid of her repugnant husband.

Thomas readily agreed to the plan; he hated the master along with many others in the household. His 14-year-old daughter Emma, who had been a serving maid at the Hall, had become a victim of his master's lust and made pregnant by him. Afraid and overcome with shame, she had run away. Thomas had searched high and low for Emma, until he eventually found her scrubbing floors in a workhouse many miles away, where he was informed that her prematurely born baby boy had been given up for adoption.

Thomas had brought his sobbing daughter home, and later that day she had told her parents that she was going for a stroll in the meadow. A neighbour had later arrived at his door to inform them that Emma had been found floating in the river.

Thomas and his wife were heartbroken; he would never forget looking down at her drenched, pitiful remains lying on the riverbank. His once vibrant daughter, Emma, was dead and nothing would ever bring her back. With a heavy heart, he had picked her up and taken her home so that his wife could prepare her body for burial.

Because it was suicide, it was said that Emma had brought shame upon her parents and evil to the village. Therefore, there would be no prayers or service held for Emma, and she would have to be buried in unconsecrated ground away from the vicinity of the cemetery and church.

Thomas and his sobbing wife prayed and watched as Emma's body was lowered into the pauper's grave by a small group of family members. Thomas cursed Samuel Goldberg for the degradation he had wrought upon his family.

He vowed that one day he would carry out his own retribution against the man who had ruined his daughter and brought shame upon his family.

It wasn't until Hannah's voice broke into his anguished thoughts that he began to understand what she was asking of him.

As soon as the staff were dismissed, Hannah and Thomas quickly retreated to the upstairs bedroom where her husband lay groaning on the bed. Then with Hannah's approval, Thomas struck a heavy blow to Samuel's head with his clenched fist, ensuring that he would remain unconscious for a good hour. He next bound Samuel's feet and hands with rope then gagged him with a pillowcase. As soon as he was satisfied that Samuel was completely helpless, Thomas then dragged him into the opposite bedroom, where under Hannah's instruction, he crammed Samuel into a chest and locked the lid to prevent him from escaping. Hannah then locked the bedroom door and went downstairs to await the arrival of the police to take the three inebriated men away.

When the police finally arrived, Hannah sent for Sarah, Elizabeth's maid, to give her testimony of what she had seen and heard, but to omit her husband's presence in the perverted attack.

Meanwhile, as the rest of the staff were being questioned, Sarah and Maria had taken two of the officers and shown them where they had hidden the stained linen from Elizabeth's bed after the attack.

Other officers had been taken upstairs by the butler and shown into the master's bedroom where they shook the three naked men awake and ordered them to get dressed. Despite their protests, they were placed under arrest and taken away in the paddy wagon.

Then after entering Elizabeth's bedroom and seeing her lying dead with a bruised and battered face, the police officers offered their condolences to Hannah, before returning downstairs to the lounge to ask Hannah about her husband's whereabouts. Hannah told them she had no idea of where he had gone, and called for Peter the stable lad, whom she had earlier advised about what to say to the police.

Peter, the stable boy who had ridden out to inform Hannah of what was occurring back at the manor, said that Samuel hadn't bothered to saddle his horse. He had ridden out at a gallop and headed out onto the moors, that was all he knew of his master's whereabouts.

"Perhaps it's his way of dealing with grief," one officer said sympathetically.

"Or maybe he was feeling guilty about something as bad as this happening in his own home, especially while he was there," Thomas quipped sarcastically.

Hannah didn't say a word, she just nodded her head in agreement.

It was later discovered by Hannah that Elizabeth had drunk every drop of laudanum from the bottle that Hannah always kept by her bedside to use as a sleeping potion.

Before she had died, Elizabeth had written a letter to her mother describing every abomination of what her father and his friends had done to her. She specifically detailed that her father was determined to make her pregnant so that the pure line of the Goldberg family would be carried on from the union with his own daughter and not from the upstart she was hoping to marry.

To Elizabeth's disgust, he had even told her that he was the son of his own father, who along with Samuel had constantly copulated with Hannah until she became pregnant by either one of them, hoping that the child would be a boy so that he could carry on the tradition of the family name and that the bloodline would remain pure.

Hannah didn't dispute this as she had been forced into a loveless marriage of convenience and ever since her daughter's birth, she wouldn't let Samuel nor his father near her. She had never forgiven him for allowing the disgraceful acts that had been forced upon her.

Afterwards, Elizabeth had written in her diary, giving the same details she had written in the letter to her mother. Elizabeth had then hidden the diary, along with her engagement ring, beneath her wedding gown, diamond tiara, veil and all the accessories. She then locked them in her wedding trousseau chest and had hidden the key in a crack inside the ingle nook fireplace before lying down to die. The chest containing her trousseau had been taken up into the attic by Thomas, where no one was allowed to touch it. Thomas had fitted two solid locks on the attic door so that the trunk would remain there and be left undisturbed over the years.

Chapter 4
A Mother's Revenge

Blinded by fury, Hannah ordered three of the stable men to gather together a large number of blocks of stone and take them down to the farthest end of the cellar.

As soon as the task was completed, Thomas went out into the backyard to bring the heavy-duty wheels inside the Hall, he then hauled them up the servants' staircase and across the landing to where Hannah was waiting to unlock the door of the bedroom where her husband lay incarcerated in the packing trunk.

Together, they heaved the trunk onto the wheels and once it was loaded, Thomas pushed it down the staircase and along the corridor to the cellar door where he banged it unceremoniously, one step at a time, down the down the thirteen solid stone steps until reaching ground level.

Hannah led the way swinging the oil lamp from side to side so they could see where they were treading. She would however stop at various intervals to light the oil lamps that were suspended by large iron hooks in the wall. Nevertheless, although he was thankful of the extra light, Thomas felt his skin crawl and shuddered with the knowledge that they were about to cement the master into one of the tiny rooms in the cellar. He had no intention of stopping himself from carrying out the intended mission that he felt was owed to his mistress, to himself and to his dead daughter's memory.

He did however, have to duck occasionally to stop himself from banging his head on the low stone arches, and the only sound heard in the weird silence was broken by the rattling noise of the iron wheels of the cart as it clattered along the stone-flagged floor.

Without a word, Thomas trundled along through the shadowy darkness behind his mistress until reaching the furthest point of the cellar where she stopped and pointed into a freezing cold, small window less cell with an iron barred gate. Hannah then told Thomas where he should place the trunk. Thomas pushed the cart inside the cell and dropped the trunk onto the ground; where he propelled it into the far corner behind the wall where no one could see it. He then gave the trunk a hefty kick and stood waiting by the door for further instructions.

"Thomas," Hannah called, "bring the light over here then I can see what I am doing."

Thomas did as she asked and held the light alongside her and watched as they stood together in the darkness united by the hatred of Samuel Goldberg. Thomas couldn't help but admire the small slender woman's courage as she stood beside the trunk for a few moments, before taking the key from her pocket. She then unlocked the lid and threw it back in order to gaze down at her husband's naked tethered form.

As he lay helpless and shivering from both cold and fear, Hannah gave a cold heartless smile and drew the silk embroidered shawl closely around her shoulders. She then tucked the fine hand-woven pale blue lace of the cuffs of her dress into the sleeves of her satin gown.

Samuel, grateful for the fresh air, pleaded with his eyes to be released, but instead of releasing his bonds, he saw in her hand was a sharp, serrated, double-edged, glistening knife.

"Oh God," he screamed, but only a muffled sound came from his gagged mouth as Hannah leant over and grasped his flopping penis in her hand. She then lifted the defiling organ and stretched it as far as she could and despite his agonising muffled cries, she slowly sliced through the flesh and dropped it onto his belly.

Thomas felt the contents of his stomach rise into his throat when he stared in disbelief at what she was doing, and had to turn away as blood spurted from the wound where she had separated his offensive penis and watched with smug satisfaction as Samuel's body arched then dropped and lay still.

Hannah, however, wasn't done yet; she dripped cold water onto Samuel's face from the small flask that she was carrying and waited until he groaned as he regained consciousness. She then reached down and put her hand between Samuel's legs and lifted his testicles, where without a qualm, she sliced them from his body and placed the still warm bleeding flesh alongside his penis before plunging the knife deep into Samuel's heart. She then dropped the knife into the trunk and closed the lid of Samuel's final resting place and locked it.

"He won't be destroying any more lives now," she said grimly turning to Thomas, who was standing speechless by her side. "Come on, man, pull yourself together, we came down here to a do job so let's get on with it."

"I'm going to send Peter to help you, but do not speak of what we have done," she added, stooping and picking up an old rag to wipe the blood from her hands and throwing it onto the lid of the trunk, then carefully pulled the delicate lace over her hands from her sleeve.

"Yes Ma'am, No Ma'am," Thomas stammered, unable to think clearly, yet inside feeling a grim sense of satisfaction at what had been done.

Hannah was right; from now on his lordship would not be degrading anymore young women and children in his debauched orgies. Thanks to Hannah, Thomas could feel the inner strength that he had lost after the death of his only daughter surge through him.

Nevertheless, the memory and the sorrow that Lord Goldberg had caused his family to suffer would remain deeply etched in his mind forever. He would never forgive nor forget the suffering the man had caused his daughter and her mother to go through.

Within the short space of time, it had taken to remove Goldberg from this life, Thomas felt as if the whole burden of a lifetime had been lifted from his shoulders.

Hannah's words were a great inspiration to him.

Chapter 5
The Final Resting Place

"What do you want me to do?" a voice echoed eerily in the darkness, just a short distance away from Thomas.

"Eh," Thomas jumped. For a moment, he was startled and turned, holding the lamp high, he was relieved to see Peter emerging from the dark shadows of the cellar.

"Her ladyship has asked me to help you build a doorway up, but for the life of me I can't understand why." Peter stood shaking his head in confusion. "We could have stored some of those pots in there," he grumbled pointing towards the less than normal sized room.

"They say that old judge, Ezra Goldberg, used to have prisoners awaiting execution kept down here," he added smugly, as if knowing something that Thomas didn't already know. "Because there's locks on all these barred doors down here, and what do you think is behind that door?" pointing to a heavy studded oak door that was built into the wall barring anyone going anything further into the remaining part of the cellar.

"I don't bloody know, do I?" Thomas snapped, thankful that he had placed the chest out of sight behind the wall.

"I suppose they could have at some time. Hey now, wait a minute," he added thoughtfully rubbing the hairy bristle on his chin. "Come to think of it, old Albert did mention something to me a few years back. The Goldbergs had always been judges and this is Gallows Hill, yes that's it," he replied suddenly recalling what Albert had told him shortly before the old man died.

"They were called the hanging Judges, and the courthouse was only a short walk away from the Hall. The condemned prisoners were locked away behind that door. Old Albert said that the locals got sick and tired of innocent people being incarcerated there waiting to be hung. The Goldbergs didn't care if they were innocent or guilty, the poor sods were either hung or sent here to rot in the miserable prison dungeons behind that door. They imprisoned mostly young women and children down here, that's why all of these cell gates lock and there are no windows. They were prison cells."

"By heck, I'd forgotten about that."

"Well, I am good for something," Peter responded with a cocky grin.

"Shut up and get on with the job," Thomas said giving him a crack at the back of his head. "I've already taken the gate and frame off so let's get cracking, the sooner we get the job done, the sooner we're out of here. It's always bloody cold down here," he grumbled, rubbing his bulging muscular arms.

"We've got all the stuff we need down here, and there's two water faucets fitted in the wall with buckets hung beneath them, so we don't have to worry about mixing the lime mortar. All we need now is to find it, plus the shovels for mixing and a trowel for laying the stones. So let's find what we need then we can get the job done and get out of here."

Thankfully, four male members of staff always made sure that everything was sorted and placed in its correct order and stored in their rightful places. They also ensured that the cellar floor was swept clean. Most of the smaller items had been packed and stored in the small cells that were aligned along the walls of the cellar. The area to the left corner of the cellar was directly alongside the steps where the large stone walled coal bunker was situated and always kept filled with coal.

Alongside of this was a stone enclosure for the logs to be stored and kept dry during the winter months.

Close to this was the first cell containing stone shelves where candles and lighters were kept, also extra lamps for enabling any member of the household to read or write in the dark wintry months. In the adjacent cell large vats of oil were stored for lighting the lamps.

Each of the small cells contained articles of use to the household, nevertheless the few lamps that Hannah had lit couldn't compensate for the eerie sensations the two men were experiencing in the grim darkness of the cellar. When both suddenly underwent a strong sense of unease and felt that someone was following close behind as they searched from one area to another for the equipment they needed.

The dark, gloomy atmosphere and the miniscule lighting that came from the two single oil lamps they were using forced Thomas and Peter to stay close together. Especially when the poor lighting from the lamps they were carrying cast weird shadows dancing eerily around them.

"Thomas! Thomas! Come take a look at what I've found here," Peter called softly as if he was afraid of disturbing something or someone they couldn't see.

Thomas hurried to his side and peered over his shoulder.

"What is it lad? What have you found?" he asked, holding the lamp high.

"Look," Peter pointed to a stone ledge, "there's over a dozen good-sized oil lamps on that shelf, and it looks like there's still some oil left in them."

Thomas could hardly believe their luck when seeing a number of rusty old oil lamps that had been discarded but were still in good working order, plus a fire steel they could use to light the contents of the tinder box. They would then transfer the flame to the candle by using a wooden splint. Also laid on the stone slab, were dozens of mixed sized candles that would come in useful whenever necessary.

Thomas knew there was already a number of drums stored near the bottom of the staircase filled with oil for the household use, therefore he could fill the extra lamps with oil and give himself more-light to see what he was doing when sealing the doorway. Also, with additional light they would be able them to find the items they needed; lime mortar, shovels, trowels, hammers and chisels.

"Come on lad, let's get this stuff moved," Thomas said gruffly. "We can take these lamps and get them lit then we can see what we're doing."

Meanwhile, Hannah had gone upstairs, and after checking that no one was about in the kitchen, she hastily prepared bread, meat and cheese and two flagons of beer for Thomas and Peter, which she placed on a silver tray and carried down into the cellar for them.

"You shouldn't be carrying this, ma'am, it's too heavy; besides, it's a servant's job not yours," Thomas reprimanded taking the tray from her.

"It's alright," she whispered, then turned and made her way back up the steps.

Thomas and Peter rested for only short periods of time to eat and drink, but hadn't realised that it was almost midnight before they had completed the task they'd been given. They next thoroughly cleaned the area where they had been working and replaced the tools in the areas where they had found them, making it appear that nothing had been disturbed.

Nevertheless, Peter was more than satisfied when Hannah returned and pressed a gold sovereign into his hand.

"Do not tell anyone where you have been and what we have done," Thomas warned. "Or you will not live to enjoy spending it."

Peter stepped back, staring open-mouthed at Thomas then to Hannah.

"You know I won't," he stammered, unaccustomed to Thomas using a threatening stance.

"Good, now be off with you," Thomas said giving him a kick up the backside as he scurried away.

"Take this purse and thank you, Thomas, for what you have done for me this day," Hannah said, thankful for the darkness to hide the tears in her eyes.

"Thank you, my lady," Thomas replied when feeling the weight of the coins in the purse. "But you needn't have paid me," he said in a solemn tone. "You know that you can always count on me to help, and that I don't always want—"

"Please don't say anymore." Hannah then nodded and turned away to return up the cellar steps to her rooms. Where she allowed herself to give a sigh of relief and poured a glass of port then raised it in a salute.

"To my absent husband," she announced, flopping down into a chair and allowing herself to feel a sense of relief at getting rid of her revolting, incestuous husband.

Chapter 6
The Aftermath

In the months that followed, Hannah gave the tied cottages and a plot of land to work, to the people who had toiled there for many years. She next sold the Hall to a private individual. A vast acreage of the land that she owned was sold to a man on the understanding that he would develop a new village and a factory where the local people would find homes and work. She then moved as far away as possible from the area where she had suffered so much torment from her abusive husband, and the distressing memory of her daughter's death.

After a time however, a Lord Saltzberg who had purchased the Hall ran into debt and deliberately set fire to the building. But in doing so it was believed that he had perished in the fire, along with six of his friends, one stormy evening while in a drunken orgy. Three quarters of the building collapsed into the cellars and now lay in ruins, leaving only the main part of the Hall, being saved from the flames.

The property had then lain in ruins for a number of years, before a retired major came along and purchased the property that he refurbished for his wife and family. He didn't stay very long however, after his wife and two sons died tragically. His sons were drowned in a boating accident, and his wife's death was attributed to falling down the cellar steps and breaking her back. But before she died, she was adamant that she had been pushed by a man who disappeared through the wall in the cellar. Her husband put her comments down to the rantings of a woman whose mind was clouded by the drugs she had been given to kill the pain before her death.

But the servants thought differently; they had also seen something moving about down there and were afraid to venture into the cellar alone. The Major was so distressed by the loss of his family that he left the Hall and sold it.

Throughout the years, Goldberg Hall had many owners, but its unlucky reputation preceded it. The Hall had achieved such a notorious reputation of hauntings that it stopped prospective buyers from purchasing the property. The latest owners, who had dismissed the idea of ghosts, soon changed their minds and fled after witnessing more than one figure moving about the Hall and hearing unearthly screams echoing around the building. After that, the Hall became known as being both haunted and cursed and no one would dare venture near it, and it acquired the name: Goldberg Cursed Hall.

Many years later, a letter from Lady Goldberg that had been kept in the bank's vaults stating that it was not to be opened until after her death, was handed to the Mayor. The letter declared the terrible truth of the horrific atrocities of her husband Lord Goldberg and his associates and it was finally revealed to the public what he had done to his own precious daughter.

The humiliation of the rape that would have forced an unwanted pregnancy on the poor girl and the thought of bearing her own father's child was too much to bear. To hide her shame, she had taken the only way out, and that was death, she had poisoned herself by overdosing on Laudanum.

Lady Goldberg had insisted that her letter be read out and declared to the public about what had taken place to her beloved daughter on that fatal night. Due to Sarah's and Maria's evidence, the three men, James Rothenhall, Victor Price and Fredrick Summers went to the gallows protesting their innocence.

At the time of Elizabeth's death, everyone was led to believe that Lord Goldberg must have been so overcome with grief by the death of his only child that he had ridden away from the scene and hidden himself away.

No one ever knew what happened to him, it was as if he had disappeared from the face of the earth as no trace of him was never found.

Only Thomas and Hannah knew, but that was never disclosed in the letter.

Elizabeth's death had been avenged.

Chapter 7
Hilltop Grange Manor

Once again, Goldberg Hall stood empty for a number of years until Jack Armstrong, the owner of a construction company, decided to purchase the property along with a parcel of land, where he built twelve large stone dwellings at a much lower level than the Hall on Gallows Hill.

The imposing building stood at the crown of Gallows Hill overlooking the green meadow and the new development below, whereupon, after the houses were completed, Goldberg Hall was renovated and Jack renamed it Hilltop Grange Manor.

During the renovation, Jack decided to keep the original Victorian fixtures and fittings, plus much of the furniture that had been acquired by various owners over the years. This he'd had restored and returned to the house as the furnishings accentuated the different period of time since the Hall had been built. If, however, the furnishings would not be needed by the prospective buyers, then the contents of the manor would be taken away and stored. The historic society claimed that the building being a Grade 1 listed building should be preserved and its contents placed in an area for safekeeping as they were of historic value.

The frontage of the Hall had remained the same with its six, ten feet wide stone steps leading up to the door, where two massive marble statues of hand carved Mythological Dragons appeared to be guarding the entrance to the Grange. Four deeply ingrained Grecian design stone columns supported a six feet wide carved stone balustrade balcony that spanned across the full length of the building fascia. The balcony protected anyone when the weather became extreme as they entered through the original solid oak double doors.

To the left of the door were two large rooms with bay windows, while on the right were two more corresponding bay windows. Upstairs were four more bay windows these however, were on the outside separated in the centre by a clock that not only told the time, but the month year and was encircled by signs of the zodiac and solar system.

Above all this grandeur stood two medium sized turrets that were set on either side of the building, and created an eerie atmosphere as they soared ominously upward into the misty snow filled sky.

Nevertheless, Jack Armstrong was feeling very pleased with himself, knowing that all of the hard work that he had put into rebuilding and refurbishing the mansion had finally paid off. And to ensure that the property would be saleable Jack had the whole building sandblasted to remove every grain of residue from the fire blackened stone. The extra work however, had cost him more than he'd expected. Nevertheless, through the falling snow, the building now stood proud and clean, thanks to Jack.

However, while waiting for the new owners to arrive, Jack for some inexplicable reason had suddenly felt uncomfortable inside the warm luxurious surroundings. He decided that although it was warmer inside the Grange, he would rather wait outside for the Wilsons to arrive. But once again the snow had begun falling heavily, forcing Jack to take shelter beneath the balcony.

But as he stood stamping his feet in an effort to keep warm, Jack felt himself being scrutinised and shuddered when sensing someone watching him. At first, he tried to brush it to one side knowing that he was standing too close to the building for anyone to be positioned behind him. But the weird sensation persisted and wouldn't go away.

Shit, he thought to himself, *those bloody stupid tales about ghosts are getting to me.*

But when he turned and glanced inside the house through the window behind him, Jack almost collapsed with fright when seeing the ashen face of a young woman peering at him through the glass.

How the hell did she get in there? he cursed, then felt his legs go weak when she slowly faded from his sight. Jack instinctively knew that the house was empty, he had locked all of the doors and the keys were in his pocket so no one could have been inside the Grange.

"Shit," he muttered again, "that fucking thing must have been watching me and the crew while we were working here." But his ordeal was far from over, when he suddenly perceived a numbing coldness infiltrating his entire body and within seconds, he heard the pitiful wailing of a child screaming for its mother emanating from inside the Grange.

"Holy Mother of God," he whispered through his numb lips, "I can't stand any more of this." It was then he decided to distance himself from the building.

Feeling as if his knees were turning to water, Jack stumbled through the deep snow away from the mansion, while at the same time thinking of the rumours he had heard about the Hell Fire Club orgies that had been held there in the past and the number of children who had been sacrificed in the satanic rituals.

Forcing himself to push away the unpleasant thoughts that were now ravaging his mind, Jack compelled himself to concentrate on how he'd removed the huge piles of stone that had been left at either side of the manor, where it had become overgrown with weeds and moss that had coagulated over the years and had been covering the stone blocks.

"Concentrate, man, concentrate," he shouted out loud, when the oppressive sensations began building once again inside of him.

"After we removed the fire-damaged stone and rubble from around the mansion…" without any reason, Jack began sobbing as he fought to control his mind, "we took it to the base of Gallows Hill, where it would be used for building the new houses, and the land still needed levelling out to improve the mansion's appearance."

He hesitated for a moment and with trembling hands he took his handkerchief from his pocket and blew his nose. But as he stood looking fearfully about, a strange weird aura fell around him.

What the bloody hell, Jack cursed, then dropped silent and gaped open-mouthed and couldn't stop himself from screaming when seeing the appalling figure of a starved man draped in tattered bloodstained clothing approaching him through the snow. He then stopped when reaching Jack, and for a few seconds the pair stood looking at one another before the mysterious figure disappeared from sight.

"Oh shit no, the car," he cried fighting to control the fear that had built within him, "let me get into my car."

Sweating from sheer fright, Jack hurried down the gravel path to where he had parked his battered old Land Rover near the evergreen bushes, he had parked to give more space for the removal men's vehicles when unloading the new owner's belongings.

In a blind panic, Jack jumped inside as soon as he reached the vehicle and locked the door.

"Why couldn't the bloody estate agent be here to meet them instead of me? For God's sake it's only a bit of fucking snow. Where was I?" he mumbled trying to concentrate on anything but what he was feeling.

"Oh yes, the landscape gardener I hired, he planted the varied trees and bushes to the left of the building." Jack glanced anxiously outside into the blanket of falling snow, hoping nothing was out there waiting for him to make the wrong move, and wondering what the hell was wrong with him, he had never lost control of his emotions before, nor had he felt at such a loss as he did now.

The next thing he did to help distract himself was to fumble under the dashboard and pull out a copy of the original plans of the old Hall. Recalling that he had found it strange that the extensions to the building in the past had been erected in one direction only, and that was straight back behind the Hall. Jack had decided that a lawned area with spectacular ornamental gardens and colourful flowerbeds would be appropriate at the rear and right-hand side of the property. These though were now quickly disappearing beneath the continuous downpour of falling snow.

Jack had been annoyed when, as the Hall was a Grade A listed building, he had been forced to get planning permission from the Council to remove the broken sashed windows that had been shattered by vandals, these had to be replaced with sashed double-glazed units.

At that moment though, the bays were draped with icicles and snow giving a sinister and austere frosty sense of dismissal to anyone who approached the manor house. But once inside, the warmth from the building gave out a welcoming impression. To Jack however, it was now a false welcoming impression.

Jack looked at his watch, 10:40 it read. "They should have been here at 10:15," he grumbled, "they must have been held up by the snow; I'll give it another ten minutes then I'm off, I've had enough."

Jack glanced into his driving mirror and felt his heart stop. He let out a scream of terror when he saw what was reflected in the mirror, sitting behind him.

Chapter 8
The Interior of the Grange

Jack and the architects had worked hard together to stay within a sensible budget and had given a new spectacular lease of life to the old Hall now renamed The Grange. Separating the large entrance from the interior of the hall stood a pair of wide, tall double doors.

These consisted of thick etched glass set above a sturdy oak lower section that was designed to impress the constant stream of visitors to the hall. On either side of the doors were decoratively carved wooden panels, from where a long corridor led into a wide circular area.

The ground floor was a spacious expanse with long, polished wooden floors and an intricately arched wooden trellised ceiling. There were eight mahogany doors along the corridors that led in various directions, four of the doors led to the front rooms of the hall, while the other four to the rear of the house. This was where an elegant, modern fitted kitchen, complete with an Aga cooker and a luxurious dining area was set. To the rear of the kitchen was a utility and storage facility where cupboards and shelving lined the walls.

The corridors adjoining the rooms were covered with antique mahogany carved panels and low wattage lamps fitted at alternate distances. The panels at one time had been covered with mould that had built up over the years of neglect and had settled on each carving. But thanks to Jack, they had been carefully removed and restored to their former glory.

Jack had to fight with the planners to fit the whole of the house with central heating. To keep the antique panelling from warping and the antique furniture at a specific heat so as not to cause any further damage to the priceless objects, it was finally agreed that the spacious rooms and lengthy corridors would be fitted with underfloor heating rather than with radiators.

Antique tables and chairs lined the corridor leading to the four bay windowed front rooms, two were set on either side of the entrance to the main area of the house. The bay windows gave a wide ceramic view of the spectacular gardens.

To the right, at the rear of the house was a magnificent room specifically designed for entertaining guests, this at one time had been used as a ballroom in where extravagant dances and dinner parties had been held. When Jack had first purchased the property, he had noticed that the original maple floor was covered with debris and leaves that had collected there over the years.

As luck would have it, the wooden floor hadn't warped, and to keep the continuity of the house, Jack had ensured that the floor had been cleaned and polished to a smooth lustrous finish.

The only access to the ballroom was through two wide etched glass doors exiting onto the corridor. Above the floor the original exotically decorated ceiling and cornice remained intact and needed only a few minor repairs to cover the cracks caused by damp. Hanging from the ceiling were two massive breath-taking hand-cut crystal chandelier. These had been removed at an earlier time by the historic society to preserve them from being damaged or stolen by dropouts and drug addicts who were constantly breaking into derelict properties.

Set in the lower part of the walls were light mahogany sculptured timber panels, and above the panelling the walls had been painted a delicate shade of peach. Beautiful crystal wall lights were set alternately about the ballroom, these were of the same quality crystal as the chandeliers suspended above. In the centre of the ballroom were two huge, sliding glass panelled doors that could be closed to create two separate areas enabling the space to become more functional.

This room was overlooking a beautiful rose garden complete with a small lake. Adding to the picturesque scenery was a natural waterfall fed from the nearby river. This cascaded down over the large rocks that had lain there for many years.

Behind the utility room and ballroom were two other rooms that were centrally placed and separated by a wide corridor; these two rooms were the games rooms where Gerry had placed two billiards tables with all the fittings for his friends to enjoy, plus dart boards and a bar with plush seating all around. The other games room was kitted out with a piano and tables to accommodate backgammon, chess and a multitude of games for the ladies, and a small kitchenet and bar. This was where the women could chat without the interruption of nosy men.

On either side of these rooms, were spacious open areas with four huge stone pillars supporting the rooms above. Jack assumed that in the past these would have been the orangeries where the ladies would meet and sit amongst the flowers to talk when the weather was either too wet or cold for them to venture outside. These areas were now devoid of all plants and vegetation.

Leading from the large circular area at the centre of the Hall, was a wide sweeping mahogany staircase complete with the originally carved balustrade. Set on each side of the staircase handrail were two large hand carved mahogany dragons, these Jack later discovered were the family's insignia. The staircase must have been at least ten feet wide that led up towards the balcony, and swept in two directions along either side of the first floor landing.

The balcony led along a corridor to each of the bedrooms, four at the front and four behind. A Victorian bathroom was situated at either end of the balcony. The balcony then turned at the rear of the corridor with another staircase leading up to the attic.

Behind the four bedrooms were two more centrally placed rooms with a long corridor running on either side of them. Inside these rooms each had an extra door that opened onto a spacious open area that was surrounded by heavy cast iron railings.

The bedrooms for the family's use were of a larger size than normal, and Jack had each bedroom fitted with its own end suite and walk-in wardrobe. The extra door fitted each room's central point led to another room that could be used as somewhere for the children to study while at home from school or college. Or where they could watch their own choice of TV programs and play computer games.

This had been a big sales advantage, when a young family had come to view the Grange house five weeks previously, immediately they had viewed the property the couple had made the decision to purchase it and had never questioned why the asking price was so low, when compared to the newer counterparts.

Jack felt that it was best if he said nothing of the Hilltop Grange Manor's past history, and thought the least said the better. They would find out soon enough.

Jack had informed them that beneath the grange was the low stone arched cellar with small cells on either side. The furthest point had been sealed off due to the damage that had been caused by the fire. When at its height most of the building's structure had been destroyed and had collapsed into the cellar. But the remaining area of the cellar beneath the Grange was still quite large and dry therefore it was ideal for storage purposes.

Jack then pointed out that this was where the central heating boiler was situated and the fuse boxes and that each box for every individual room was listed. This would make it easier for them to find whatever item had fused if they ever had an electrical problem. Also, coal and logs were stored there that could be used for the fires in the ingle-nook fireplaces; that was if they had a bad winter and needed the extra warmth.

Nevertheless, the couple with the three young children who had first viewed the property had fallen in love with the house and were about to move in that very day.

Chapter 9
Moving into the Grange

"I hope it isn't going to be much further," Ava moaned, crossing and uncrossing her legs. "I'm dying for a wee."

"It's only about a mile up the road now," her husband Gerry Wilson replied, turning his rugged good-looking face towards her. "But I can pull up if you're that desperate and—"

"No way," she interrupted testily, "I'm not squatting down for all and sundry to see. Besides…" she said, giving a shudder as she looked through the windscreen at the bleak open countryside, "it's snowing, and if you look properly, you will notice that the snow has drifted here and it's deep, so there's no way I'm dropping my pants out there. I'd freeze to death if I did."

"Shit," he grumbled, when a massive tractor pulled out of a nearby gate, blocking the road ahead and began trundling slowly forward, showering the car windscreen with sludge and muck from the field. "Bloody hell! I can't see a dammed thing!" he snarled as the wipers fought to clear the filth that was being thrown up and blocking his vision.

"Get out of the bloody way!" Gerry shouted, blowing his horn in frustration, oblivious to the fact that the farmer couldn't hear a thing due to the thunderous roar from the tractor's engine.

To Gerry's relief, the tractor pulled off the road into a nearby lane and headed towards a farm.

"Thank goodness for that," he griped.

His tone suddenly changed when the Grange Manor came into view. "Look Ave, the house, you can see it now. My god it looks even bigger than it did when we first saw it."

Ava peered through the falling snow where she saw their new home coming into view.

"The reason why it looks bigger, you idiot, is because all of the skips have been removed from the front."

Gerry threw her a withering glance but didn't respond to her scathing remark, and flashed the car's headlights towards the stocky, medium height Jack, who was stood huddled from the cold and falling snow in his leather work boots, fleece-lined sheepskin jacket and peaked cap, awaiting their arrival.

As soon as Gerry pulled up in front of the house, Ava had leapt out of the car and was racing towards the door, where to her dismay she found that it was locked.

"Quick, unlock the door," she yelled at Jack, "I need the loo, fast."

Jack smiled at the urgency in her voice as he reached into his pocket and unlocked the front door then stepped back, allowing Ava to hastily push past him and make a beeline for the toilet.

Gerry, meanwhile, had parked his four-wheel drive black Range Rover out of the way of the two removal vans that were now drawing up outside the front door. They were met by a much calmer Ava, who told them where to place the downstairs furniture.

Jack couldn't help but admire his slim, delicately built 32-year-old wife, who was still as beautiful as the day they met, a green-eyed, fiery-tempered redhead who always got her own way. And despite her short stature of five feet two, Ava was always in complete control of whatever she did.

Gerry, her husband, however, was a completely different person, he was a patient steel grey blue-eyed man who had the physical stature of a six-and-a-half-foot athlete. In the past, Gerry had been a professional rugby player, but a knee injury had finished his career in the game. Therefore, he had concentrated on a career and was building up a strong reputation as an architect. His dark medium length wavy hair that he usually wore in a ponytail fell across his face as he concentrated on lifting the boxes he had placed in the back of his black Range Rover. These boxes contained electrical equipment, private files and records that were essential for his and Ava's work.

At that moment, their friend David, who ran a private detective agency with his partner, Bob, pulled up alongside him in Ava's brand new, pale blue Mercedes four-wheel drive car. Gerry had insisted that she purchase the diesel car as they would be living in a rural area. Then, when the weather turned, she would be able to get to wherever she needed to go in a sensible motor vehicle.

David, however, had been grateful for the vehicle he was handling, when at times he felt the car skid on the snow and ice-filled potholes on the uneven rough road. He had watched in his rear-view mirror as Bob struggled behind to control his own vehicle that they would be using for their return journey. Thankful that it was a sturdy older model Volvo that had been built to last.

Meanwhile, Ava had noticed the strange looks on the removal men's faces and whispers that passed between them, when she had instructed them in which rooms the beds, furniture and storage boxes should be placed. She was also aware of their reluctance to enter the front bedroom and set the four-poster bed that was already in there to where she wanted it positioned.

"I wouldn't sleep in that bed, nor that front bedroom," Joe whispered to Bert.

"No, and neither would I, in fact I wouldn't live here, not for all the tea in China," Bert replied. "They say it's as haunted as hell."

Ava had pretended to be busy by placing some of the children's belongings in their rooms, but she couldn't help overhearing some of the comments that Joe and Bert were making to one another.

Nor the strange looks that passed between them when she asked that they reposition the four-poster bed in the second bedroom. The bed had been placed too close to the corner wall, whereupon the person sleeping in there would have to clamber over his or her partner to get in and out of bed.

Ignoring their comments and excuses to leave the upstairs rooms, Ava proceeded to tell the men where to place the furniture in the boys' rooms and where to place the boxes which she would unpack herself when they had more time.

She was pleased however that the new mats had arrived and were now being spread about the solid oak floors, along with the large Asian silk mats from the house itself that were in keeping with the Grange. These had been cleaned and placed in storage until purchased by Gerry and Ava.

The warmth filling every room of the house came from the new central heating system that was established in the cellar, this supplied the entire building of the spacious manor with the necessary warmth that was needed during the cold winter period. On the ground floor levels, the original Ingle nook fireplaces had been restored, and had logs stacked safely on either side of the fire place. The logs were safely contained in a sealed area away from any sparks that could ignite them and start an unnecessary fire.

Gerry in the meantime had gone upstairs to check that the children's new beds were placed and set up in their chosen rooms, along with the boxes of electrical equipment, books toys, and whatever else they would be needing. On their first visit to the Grange, the two boys, twelve-year-old Arnold and David thirteen, had chosen the back bedrooms. Each of these rooms were large enough to accommodate two, three-quarter-sized beds, two reclining chairs plus a medium-sized table with four matching chairs. The smaller room connecting their sleeping quarters would be used for their computer and games console and books for school studies.

Sally, their 9-year-old daughter, had chosen a room at the front of the house, with a wide cushioned bay window overlooking the gardens. All of the accessories were identical to her brothers' two separate bedrooms. The reason for all three children having extra beds in their rooms was to accommodate their friends when staying overnight.

Jenny had also purchased two new antique-designed double beds and placed them in each of the guest rooms. The beds and furniture from her old home were placed in two of the other bedrooms.

And some of the furniture from their old home that was deemed unnecessary had been assigned to the spare room at the rear of the extra upstairs bedrooms. This was already packed away and covered with dust sheets. All three children, who were staying for a week with their aunt Caroline, had stern instructions from their father that on their return home the following day, there must be no running on the balcony or climbing and sliding down the staircase banister rails.

Chapter 10
Jack

Ava gave a sigh of relief when the removal men had left.

"Thank goodness they've gone," she said flopping down onto a chair. Ava was exhausted from all of the hustle and bustle of the move.

Gerry came and sat beside her. "I don't ever want to move again after this, I'm buggered."

"Don't swear, Gerry, I don't want the children picking up that sort of language. By the way, did you see where Jack went? I was going to give him a cup of tea; he looked frozen."

"Come to think of it, no, he must have gone home, it is cold out there."

Gerry got up and walked over to the window and glanced outside. "I can't see him. As I said, he must have gone home. Thank goodness for that though," he said turning towards Ava.

"Thank goodness for what?"

"The snow, it's nearly stopped."

"Well go see if Jack's outside and bring him in."

"But I'm just starting to get warmed through."

"Gerry, go see if he wants a drink of something, he wasn't looking very well when he met us at the door."

"Oh, for goodness sake," he grumbled, glaring at her, then turned and strutted out of the lounge and down the hall towards the cloakroom where he'd hung his coat.

"See you shortly," he called, sending a draft of cold air through the hall when he opened the door and stepped outside. Gerry stood for a while under the balcony repeatedly calling Jack's name but there was no reply. He did notice though, that his battered old Land Rover was still parked where he had left it over by the bushes.

"Well, he's got to be somewhere nearby, his vehicle's still here and the engine's running." Gerry muttered to himself.

Peering through the lightly falling snow, Gerry could just make out a figure in the driver's seat through the frosted glass but it wasn't moving. Instinctively, Gerry sensed that something was wrong and hurried across the drive to where Jack's vehicle was parked and rubbed at the glass to see inside.

"Oh no! Dear God no," he exclaimed loudly when seeing Jack's frozen body with his gloved hands still clutching the steering wheel, and a look of abject terror on his face.

"Jack!" He shouted. "Jack, come on man, open the fucking door," he called, frantically pulling at the door handle.

The look of intense fear on Jack's deathly frozen face filled Gerry with a petrifying dread. He knew that he was wasting his breath shouting. Even so Gerry couldn't help but yell again for Jack to open the door as he wrenched at the handle, but he couldn't move it, it was locked from the inside.

"Jack! Jack!" he yelled, banging on the window with his fist, but still there was no movement from inside. "I've got to get him out of there," was all Gerry could think of at that moment. "Perhaps it's not too late."

In panic, Gerry looked around for something to break open the vehicle's window and raced over to the rockery where he grabbed a lump of stone. Then he hurried back to the car and smashed it through the glass and forced his hand inside to unlock the door. But when Gerry reached over and touched Jack, he quickly withdrew his hand when discovering that Jack's body was a frozen mass of ice. By all appearances, Jack looked as if he had been dead for days, never mind minutes or hours.

Chapter 11
The Police Investigation

Numb with shock, Gerry raced into the house where he threw his wet jacket and muddy boots down onto the floor, then hurried to the kitchen where Ava was pouring herself a second cup of tea.

"Call the police and an ambulance," he shouted, "now!"

"What? What is it? What's happened?" she stammered.

"Never mind the questions; just do as I say."

With trembling hands, Ava picked up the kitchen phone and dialled the emergency services telling them to come to the Manor immediately as there had been a terrible incident.

Before the operator could ask any questions, Ava replaced the phone then hurried to Gerry who was sobbing and shaking like a leaf.

"What is it? Has something happened to Jack?" she asked in a shaky voice as she handed him the drink of tea.

"He's dead."

"What! He can't be. We were only talking to him a short while ago."

"Please Ava, no more questions." he said burying his head in his hands. "I can't take any more right now."

Stunned by what Gerry had told her, Ava hurried over to the cabinet took out the bottle of whiskey and poured it into a tumbler before handing it to Gerry. Then in silence, she seated herself beside her husband and held his shaking hand to await the arrival of the police and ambulance.

Within a short space of time, the police and ambulance had arrived. At the first glimpse of Jack's frozen body, the medics knew that nothing could be done for the poor unfortunate man.

They were baffled however, as to how Jack could have frozen to death as quickly as he had. They also found it rather odd that someone could freeze as solid as Jack had become in just a matter of hours.

Meanwhile, Sergeant Bennet stood in deep conversation with the medics as they considered what would be the best way to remove Jack from the vehicle without causing any damage to his body, as his hands and body were frozen to the vehicle's interior. In the end, they decided that it would be for the best if they left him where he was and called for the tow truck to take both Jack and the vehicle to the morgue where a specialist team would know how to get him out of there.

In the meantime, a number of officers were checking the surrounding area for any signs of violence, while Sergeant Bennett and Officer Clarke went inside the mansion to Interview Gerry and Ava. Ava explained that although Jack seemed to be alright when he met them at the door, he had looked a little peaky. Other than that, they hadn't seen him again until Gerry found him dead just a short while ago in his car.

"Sir," Sergeant Bennet said to Gerry as he flicked open his notebook and began writing. "What time did you say it was when you last saw the victim?"

"It was either quarter to eleven or eleven o clock,"

"That's right," Ava added, "he unlocked the door for me, but we didn't see him again after that."

"Are you certain you didn't notice him? Did he help carry anything into the house?" Sergeant Bennett asked, his eyes darting from Ava to Gerry.

"No, we were too busy checking that everything was being put in its proper place," Gerry replied testily. "Look, if you don't mind," Gerry snapped, "I've just had a lousy experience, and not only that, we have just moved in here." Gerry pointed to the boxes and cartons spread about the hall. "The cleaners will be here at three-thirty and we have to have everything in its place for our three children who will be arriving tomorrow morning, so could we call it a day. I would appreciate it if you would—"

He was about to say more when Ava interrupted him. "We can't tell you any more than we already have, so if you don't mind…"

Sergeant Bennett closed his notebook and placed it into his top pocket. "I know that the incident has been very stressful for you, and I am sorry if we have inconvenienced you, sir, madam, but you do understand that we do have to ask these questions."

The Sergeant then motioned for the constable to leave and handed Gerry a card. "If you remember anything else sir, please don't hesitate to call me on that number." He then turned and left.

Chapter 12
Reminiscing

Gerry was still in a state of shock and with Ava's advice, he had gone into his office to lie down on the leather sofa to rest for a while. She had given him two paracetamol tablets to help calm him and get rid of the blinding, stressful headache that was now plaguing him.

As he lay relaxing, he gazed out of the window and saw that the snow had begun falling heavily again and shuddered when thinking of Jack.

"The poor man," he said to himself, remembering when he and Ava had first viewed Hilltop Grange. They had been surprised to find two huge four poster beds in the front bedrooms of the house. At the time Jack had informed them that these were the only two original four poster beds to have survived the Hall's fire and neglect, along with other valuable pieces of early antique furniture that were now placed in various rooms and passages of the manor.

He had stated that if they didn't want to keep the beds then they could be taken away for safe-keeping. But if they did wish to use them, he could have mattresses and drapes made to fit the beds at an additional low cost to which Ava readily agreed. She was excited at the idea of sleeping in a four-poster bed.

In refurbishing the manor, Jack had made certain that all of the bedrooms contained their own en-suite bathrooms and walk in wardrobes plus an extra adjoining room.

Gerry closed his mind for a few moments when the painful memories of Jack being so helpful came flooding back and were almost unbearable. He suddenly found himself sobbing so hard that he almost choked on his own tears and had to push himself upright to catch his breath.

Taking his handkerchief from his pocket, Gerry wiped his eyes then blew his nose, and noticed that Ava had placed a tray containing a bottle of whiskey, bottled water and a glass on the low table nearby. He felt his hands shaking when he reached for the whiskey and opened the bottle to pour the drink then added the water and took a hearty swig in the hope that it would relax him.

Lying in the semi-darkness, Gerry recalled that when he had first taken a good look around the Manor, he had made his way up the staircase and along the balcony until he reached the front bedrooms rooms that were to become his and Ava's. Occasionally though, he had stopped when sensing someone following him but each time he had looked back, there was no one there. He had put it down to his imagination and being in a strange house.

He had continued checking out the building, and was aware that Arnold and David had commandeered the two bed rooms at the rear. Sally, on the other hand had chosen the bedroom with a bay window at the front of the house like her parents.

Two more rooms that were centrally situated behind the boy's bedrooms were long but slightly narrower than the other rooms and were totally unfurnished. Alongside each of these rooms was a dimly lit corridor leading to a blank stone wall, the wall Gerry assumed must have been built there after the fire.

But when Gerry had entered both cold empty rooms, he had noticed there was a door that, when opened, it brought him to an open balcony surrounded by ornate heavy wrought iron railings.

Through the lightly falling snow, the two balconies had given a spectacular view of the surrounding land and gardens of the property. He could also see for miles around, the village, and open farm land, and the busy motorway some fifty or sixty miles away.

Nevertheless, despite the tantalising landscape, Gerry had felt the bitter coldness biting through his clothing and had decided to return inside where it was warm and carry on exploring the rest of the house.

He became frustrated when losing his sense of direction and found himself on a dark uncarpeted curved wooden staircase that led up towards the attic. He stopped moving for a few seconds and held his breath after seeing the dark shadow of a man moving about in the darkness near the foot of the staircase.

"Who's there?" he'd called fumbling in the semi-darkness for the light switch, but there was no reply, and by the time he had managed to turn on the light, the man was gone.

"It's either my imagination or somebody is playing tricks," Gerry muttered angrily. But when he began climbing the creaking stairs towards the attic door, for some inexplicable reason, Gerry had felt a sense of unease and faltered then turned to look behind him when sensing that someone was following. He was mistaken; no one was there.

He then cursed when reaching the top of the stairs and discovered that there were two antiquated padlocks barring the attic door. The door contained two locking systems that he had never seen before, and none of the keys he held fitted them.

Gerry was furious by the time he had returned to the kitchen where Jack was speaking to Ava, and asked him about the missing keys.

To his surprise, Jack had informed him that there weren't any, even he hadn't been able to gain access to the roof from the attic. Lady Goldberg had left strict instructions in her will that the attic door must never be opened, and as it was a Grade 1 listed building, they weren't allowed to enforce entry. Therefore, the men who had been carrying out re-laying and replacing the missing stone roof slates to make the building watertight, had at times resorted to removing some of the secure slates to enable them to squeeze beneath the crawl space in order to lag the roof with a thick quality insulation material while sealing the roof.

Gerry drained his glass then lay back and tried to remember what had happened during the move.

He recalled that Ava had gone into the utility room to the left of the kitchen, to check that the fridge freezer, a free-standing tall freezer and a drinks cooler, were set in place and all working, along with the washer tumble dryer and dishwasher.

The removal men had been good enough to unload the boxes of items that needed to be refrigerated and had placed everything in the fridge. They had also unpacked the frozen fish and meat that she had packed in a number of freezer boxes and put those in the freezer.

The shelving racks and the cupboards complete with work top, had been filled with the fruit and vegetables that Ava had brought with them.

In the meantime, Gerry had commandeered one of the front magnificent high-ceilinged rooms to use as his office, and this was where he now lay in a drunken stupor. He gave a wry grin at the thought of how he had managed to build up a career of being one of the most successful architects in the whole of Yorkshire, even London was now beginning to recognise his architectural skills.

Ava on the other hand was the Editorial Editor of The Crime Writers Magazine. She had taken the adjacent room to use as her office, where she would work in the peace and quiet that was required for her to carry out her job efficiently.

As for the rooms to the right of the property, Ava had decided that one was to be used as a television room and the other purely for meditation and relaxation. They would decide what to do with the rest of space at a later date, although Gerry was planning to move his gym equipment into one of the spare bedrooms when he had enough time.

Ava had arranged for a cleaner to come to the Manor twice a week, who would also attend to the laundry and ironing as well as a window cleaner once a month and a part-time gardener in the winter months, who in the summer would be employed full time.

With these thoughts in his mind, Gerry dropped into a deep relaxing sleep.

Chapter 13
The Accident

By the time the children were due to arrive home, Ava and Gerry had everything unpacked and in its place. The children had been so excited at the thought of moving into such a grand old house that their aunt Caroline had been practically driven out of her mind with the persistent questions about the Grange's past history.

When Caroline had asked why they were so curious about the house, David told her that everyone knew that bad things had happened there and that the house was haunted. To allay their fears of a haunting, Caroline had said that it was all silly gossip and that every old house was purported to have a ghost, so they should put that silly nonsense out of their heads.

Nevertheless, the drive to Hilltop Grange had been rowdy with the children competing against one another with the new games consuls that Caroline had bought them. The two-hour drive home would have taken half an hour less, if it hadn't been for the heavy snow fall and the mist that had suddenly descended only a mile away from the Grange. By the time they had drawn closer, due to the curtain of falling snow and mist that had now become a dense fog, Caroline could hardly make out the road ahead.

It wasn't until she saw through the thick fog that directly in front of her was a huge tractor with its ploughing blades held high that she braked hard to avoid a collision. But it was too late; the car skidded and collided with the trailing plough's blades. The force of the impact immediately brought the blades dropping down and slicing through the roof of the car directly onto its four occupants; within seconds, three were dead.

The old farmer, who felt the impact, never expected seeing such carnage when he climbed from the tractor's seat and went to look at what had hit him from behind.

"Oh my god," he moaned, clutching his chest as an unexpected pain shot through him. Within seconds, he fell to the snow-covered road convulsing, then died.

"I wonder where Caroline and the children could have gotten to?" Ava asked Gerry, who was equally becoming anxious when looking out of the window and noticing the change in the weather. "They should have been here over an hour ago. She rang to say they were leaving at four pm, and now it's almost six."

"She could have broken down somewhere," Gerry snapped, irritated by his sister's irrational thinking when it came to a choice of vehicle. "You know what modern cars are like nowadays, they are always breaking down in this sort of weather. She should have bought a diesel four-wheel drive like I suggested. But no, not Caroline; instead, she bought that stupid useless thing she calls a car. I told her it was no use out here in the countryside and especially in this weather."

Ava rolled her eyes but said nothing, she'd heard those words spoken so many times before that it was like listening to an old recording.

"I'll go look for them and while I'm at it, I might as well take the towing chain in case she's skidded off the road and is stuck in a hedge bottom somewhere," he grumbled.

Without waiting for a reply, Gerry went to the hall cupboard and donned his thick winter coat, then pulled on his boots and finally his sheepskin gloves and cap.

"See you shortly," he called, slamming the door loudly behind him.

The sight of flashing blue and red lights in the distance sent shivers of apprehension down Gerry's spine when he approached a police road block. He stopped his car and wound the window down.

"What's happened?" he called anxiously, trying to see through the thick fog and blanket of snow.

The police officer came over to his vehicle. "Do you live around here, sir?" he asked.

"Yes," Gerry replied, "up the hill there."

"Do you know many people around here?"

"No, I don't, I only moved in yesterday," Gerry looked at him puzzled. "Why all the questions?"

"Are you related to anyone living in the vicinity?"

"No, I'm not. Now for goodness sake, tell me what the hell's happened!"

"It's a tractor driver sir, he's suffered a fatal heart attack and is being taken to the hospital."

Gerry nodded his head sympathetically wondering if it was the old farmer who had blocked the road a few days ago.

"I'm sorry to hear that. How long do you think the road will be closed?"

"I can't say for certain sir, but if I were you, I'd turn around and go back the way you came as this part of the road is going to be closed for a few hours yet."

"Oh, why?"

"Well sir," the officer glanced at his colleague who nodded then answered hesitantly, "a car has skidded into the back end of the tractor. Due to the force of the impact, the ploughing blades the farmer was moving to his other farm dropped on top of the car. I'm sorry to say there is only one survivor and the fire brigade are trying to cut her out."

Gerry felt his blood run cold; he unfastened his seatbelt and leapt from the car and raced to the back of the tractor. Where he saw the tangled wreckage of Caroline's car and the fire brigade frantically using cutting gear in order to dismantle the vehicle to release the surviving passenger.

"Oh no, dear god no," he screamed, when seeing through the smashed windscreen and mangled wreckage, the blood-soaked remains of his sister and eldest son who were seated in the front of the car. He realised that they must have been killed instantly, when seeing their heads were split in half by the sharp blades of the plough that had dropped from the tractor and were embedded in the bones and tissue of their bodies and skulls.

The blades had dropped onto the roof of the car then sliced through the thin cheap alloy onto the tops of their heads at a downward angle. The blades were now lodged halfway down through the centre of their blood-soaked torsos. From the head down to their abdomens, his sister and his eldest boy were literally cut in half.

In the backseat, he could just make out through the compressed debris of the car, his other son with part of the plough's blade lodged in his skull, while protruding from his daughter's head and face were shards of glass and plastic.

"My children, my children," he shrieked, pointing inside the wreckage as he tried to push past the two firemen as they worked, fastidiously trying to release his badly injured daughter.

Two police officers grabbed hold of Gerry and dragged him away from the bloody carnage.

"My children and my sister are in that car," he yelled hysterically. "Let go!" he shouted trying to break free from the men's firm grip. "I've got to help them…"

"Sir?"

Gerry spun around his eyes wild with fury, but he couldn't see anything except the horrendous bloody sight of his children and sister's bodies.

"Bring him over here, he's in shock," he heard someone saying to the officers. "Then I can explain to him what—"

"I don't need anything explaining to me, my fucking family are in that car," he shrieked wildly pulling his arms free.

"Sir, I know this is a bad shock but—"

"It is a bloody bad shock, you stupid prat."

"Please," the doctor attending the scene, said, trying to calm the distraught man. "I fully understand what you are ging through, but would you please tell me your name and where you live, and the name of your doctor? Then you can be either be taken to hospital or taken home by one of the officers."

"Home," Gerry mumbled in a daze. "Oh Christ! What am I going to say to Ava! My wife, the mother of our children."

Gerry couldn't say anymore, he collapsed sobbing into the deep snow. Through a blur of grief, Gerry gave them his name and address. He didn't notice the look that passed between the two officers, nor the incredulous expression on the doctor's face at the mention of his home, The Grange.

"Mr Wilson, can you remember your doctor's name, as both you and your wife are going to need help. What about your parents and your wife, do you have their number for us to call and let them know what has happened?"

It took Gerry a few moments to remember his parents' telephone number and their new doctor's name. They then put through an emergency call to his parents to let them know that their daughter had been involved in a motoring accident. Then they called Gerry's doctor, telling him what had occurred and asking him to get out there immediately.

In a blurred haze, Gerry could just make out what the doctor was saying as the officers helped him to his feet and assisted him into the waiting police car, before driving him home.

Chapter 14
The Aftermath

The following weeks after the funerals of their sons and Gerry's sister, Caroline, were a nightmare come true. Ava's parents Frank and Elsie arrived to take over the running of the Grange, while Ava spent every hour she could at Sally's bedside. Michael, Gerry's father, had to stay at home to take care of Helen, who had collapsed when they had been informed of the accident and the death of their only daughter Caroline.

Relatives, friends and neighbours had offered to come and stay to give them comfort, but Ava and Gerry declined their kind offers of help. They just wanted to left alone to grieve in peace over their loss. Meanwhile, Gerry had taken a month's leave of absence from his office to help him recover from the loss of his family.

Ava, who was sedated, sat in a daze both day and night by Sally's bedside clinging to the hope that she would recover from her injuries. Her pathetic little body was swathed in bandages, the intravenous drips set in both arms were secured by tapes to the cot bed rails. This was to ensure that if there was any sudden movement from Sally, then she would be unable to drag the needles from her arms. Along with this, a tracheotomy had been carried out. The tubes entering her throat allowed the mechanical machine to pump oxygen into her damaged lungs. The steady rhythmic beep, beep, of the monitors keeping Sally alive would stay in Ava's memory forever.

For a whole month, it had been touch and go as her injuries had been severe and life threatening but thankfully, due to her inner strength and the surgeon's skill, Sally was slowly regaining consciousness and to her parents' joy and relief, she was beginning to come out of the coma.

She would however, need to receive treatment in helping her communicate with people; the shock and severity of her injuries had affected her brain. Her speech had been affected along with the loss of memory. She would also need plastic surgery to repair the scars on her head, face, arms, hands and upper body, and her golden curls would eventually grow back onto her shaved head.

After a number of operations, Sally was well enough to be taken off the ventilator and breathe for herself and to sit up in bed. Ava and Gerry had tried to help Sally recover her memory by showing her family photographs in the hope that she could recognise anyone. But sadly, she had no recollection of any family members. Nevertheless, they still kept trying to bring her back to normality, she had been lucky in one sense the specialists had told them, which was she had regained all normal movements and functions of her body.

It took a further eight weeks in hospital before Sally was allowed home, where she continued with speech therapy and learning how to adapt to a new way of life. The memories of the accident were completely wiped from her memory, but the recognition of her parents began slowly returning. She couldn't however, remember the pet hamsters she had lovingly cared for as a child, nor the number of goldfish that she had named and tearfully buried in the back garden of her old home.

Sally had somehow developed an uncanny knowledge of knowing what was about to happen in the days ahead and also a worrying habit of somnambulism. This had caused her parents a great deal of anxiety, but after speaking to her physician about it, he told them not to worry. This often happened after someone had suffered traumatic injuries to the brain. He declared that in time she would grow out of it.

They were concerned however, when on the odd occasion, Gerry and Ava would hear Sally holding a conversation with someone in her bedroom. Yet when they knocked on the door and entered her room, they found that Sally was alone and assumed she had been talking to herself.

But after they left, Sally had given a sly smile and carried on entertaining her new friend whose name was Miranda. Miranda was a pretty little girl of about her own age. She had long plaited auburn hair and was dressed in an ankle length dress, white stockings and buttons down the sides of her brown boots.

As the months passed, Jenny saw a rapid increase in Sally's mental awareness, and after her tenth birthday her physician said that it would be alright for Sally to return to school. But Ava was afraid to allow her daughter out of her sight and told him that she would bring in a tutor to help with Sally's education.

The doctor had argued that Sally needed to be in the company of children her own age, and that it would be more beneficial if she got away from her present surroundings for a while.

Bearing the thought in mind, Gerry and Ava, asked Sally if she would like to return to the boarding school, St Elizabeth's, or be home tutored. Sally jumped at the chance of returning to school and to be mixing with her old class chums again. Gerry pointed out that she may not be able to recognise any of her old school friends, and that she would be moving into an upper grade.

But that didn't deter Sally, all she could talk about was returning to St Elizabeth's where she could further her education, and that she needed to gain knowledge.

Her parents could hardly believe what they were hearing, Sally had always been the one to hum and haw, at the idea of returning to school and didn't achieve as good grades as the boys. But now she could hardly wait for the days to pass so that she could return to St Elizabeth's to resume her studies.

Nevertheless, they relented and agreed to let her return to the boarding school, but not until having a word with the school governess, Miss Brocklehurst, regarding their daughter's delicate condition and state of mind. Sally must not be allowed to participate in any of the school activities where she could suffer any kind of injury, especially to her head.

Miss Brocklehurst agreed that they would not allow Sally to take any undue risks, and that her activities would be purely academic.

Once that was agreed, Sally was allowed to leave for St Elizabeth's.

Chapter 15
Strange Happenings

Four months had passed since the accident; Sally had come home from boarding school for the two weeks of Christmas holiday before she was due to return to St Elizabeth's.

In the weeks leading up to Christmas, both Gerry and Ava had reluctantly accepted invitations to parties given by their colleagues and friends. But with the depressing emotions evolving around the couple and the dispirited atmosphere that had descended upon the household, Gerry felt that he couldn't take anymore, he finally broke the grim silence while they were seated in the lounge.

"Ava," Gerry's voice broke into the miserable silence.

"What?" she responded in a sullen tone, without looking at him.

"We can't go on like this, the boys, my sister." His voice broke, Gerry couldn't say anymore.

"I agree," she mumbled with a sigh. "What do you suggest?"

"I think we should invite our parents to stay for a long weekend, not only that, but what would you say to us inviting our new neighbours at the same time to the Grange? The place needs livening up a bit, perhaps we could make it a sort of late house-warming party. You know how good you are at arranging parties. Besides, it will give you something to concentrate on and maybe take your mind away from…well, you understand what I'm trying to say," Gerry implied hesitantly.

"Gerry," Ava paused in what she was about to say.

"What?"

"I, I," she stammered.

"Come on darling, what is it?" he asked in a gentle tone. "Something else is bothering you, isn't it?"

"Yes," Ava wavered, wondering how to approach the subject. Then trying to keep the tremor from her voice, she stated in an agitated manner, "I don't know if it's my imagination or not, but I keep seeing a woman. She is old-fashioned and wears a long blue dress and elbow length silver-blue gloves; sometimes she is wearing a veil and a lace wrap around her shoulders. I've also seen another dressed in black."

Ava glanced at her husband and watched as his face suddenly took on a grim look.

"Honestly Gerry, I believe that, that I have seen a ghost."

Gerry felt a sudden cold chill run through him as he had also seen the woman on occasion but hadn't said anything to Ava as he didn't want to frighten her.

"Did you notice the colour of her hair by any chance?" he asked hesitantly, at the same time watching for her reaction.

"I couldn't see it very clearly in the shadows, but I believe it was the same colour as mine."

To Ava's relief, Gerry admitted that he had also seen the woman.

"She is usually up on the balcony watching what we are doing down here."

"That's right," Ava agreed, "and on occasion, I have seen her going towards the games' room before disappearing through the wall."

"Have you seen anything else?" Gerry asked hesitantly.

"Yes, and while we're at it, I have seen two Irish wolfhounds," she replied. "They race across the landing towards the staircase, and on other occasions, they head towards the corridor that leads to nowhere then disappear through the wall leading to the demolished part of the old Manor house."

Gerry sat nodding his head. "I've seen them as well."

"Right, now that we've gotten that out of the way and cleared the air a bit, what do you say to us having a drink and forgetting about the ghosts for now, they appear to be harmless so I can put up with them if you can." Gerry got up and went over to the cabinet and poured them both a large drink.

"Here's to a new and happier future," he said, clinking glasses with Ava.

"I think we should start living again and stop dwelling on the past; we can't do anything about it and we should be thanking our lucky stars that Sally is still with us."

He put a comforting arm around Ava's shoulders.

"Let's liven the place up a bit and have a party, we can't stay in mourning forever and we have to think about Sally, she needs company as much as we do."

To his surprise, Ava readily agreed.

"The old place does need livening up," she remarked, bursting into tears.

Gerry couldn't think of anything to say without choking up himself and gave his wife a sympathetic hug. He was missing the boys just much as she was but he had also lost his only sister whom he had loved dearly, and now wished that he had told her just how much he had cared about her.

"We do need to have people around. Do you think we should wait until Sally is back at school?" he asked.

"Yes," Ava replied, "I believe that having too many strangers around the house, and a lot of noise could upset her. There is something else bothering me though," she added.

"Who do you think she is talking to in her room?"

"Your guess is as good as mine," Gerry replied. "Do you want me to ask her?"

"No, not just yet, she may tell us in her own time."

"If you think so. When do you think I should invite our parents and neighbours to the house-warming party?" Gerry asked, changing the subject. "I could arrange it for the weekend after next when Sally is back at school, if that's alright with you."

"That's a good idea," she replied. "If you have time to print the invitations right away, then you can deliver them early. That way our neighbours will have time to make the arrangements to attend the party, and seeing as you will be near the post office, you can post the ones to our friends and colleagues."

"Great thinking," he acknowledged with a smile and gave a loving hug. "I'll get started on the printing and deliver them as soon they're ready. Is there anything you need before I go?" he asked moving towards the door. "A cup of tea, coffee?"

"No; I'm alright thanks, you go ahead and do the printing while I sort out a few papers that need looking at."

Ava turned her full attention to her work, which due to her absence had now piled up. Joanna, her second in command, had taken over the running of the company while she had been absent.

It wasn't until sometime later that Ava heard the sound of footsteps echo across the marble entrance hall and the door open behind her. Her first thoughts were that Gerry had already designed, copied and posted the invitations and was now home.

"Hello darling, you didn't take very long, did you?" she said not looking up as she continued with her typing, then felt his hand on her shoulder.

Ava stopped writing and turned; then shrieked with alarm when seeing a tall handsome man wearing a pale blue frock coat and white breeches gazing down at her; his blue eyes appeared to be searching for some sign of recognition.

"Oh my god," she cried leaping from the chair and sending it scuttling across the floor, then she fled in terror from the room.

In her panic, Ava didn't think of stopping to put on her coat, instead she raced along the passage and into the entrance hall, pulled open the door and raced from the house straight into a blanket of falling snow. Blinded by fear, Ava fled to one of the outbuildings where she found shelter under the timber-framed arched doorway of the old derelict building.

"Oh God," she quaked, unable to take her eyes away from the mansion. "What am I going to do? What am I going to do?" she sobbed, wrapping her arms around herself in an effort to protect her body from the howling wind and plummeting temperature.

At that moment Gerry returned home, where through the windscreen of the car he was shocked to see Ave standing outside, shivering, soaked to the skin and crying her eyes out.

"What the hell are you doing outside without your coat?" he shouted, stopping the car beside her. "Get in before you catch your death of cold," he yelled, leaning over and opening the car door.

Ava's teeth were chattering as she got into the car and sat without saying a word until he pulled up outside the front door.

Whereupon she became hysterical and refused to enter the house.

Chapter 16
Who's There?

While sitting in the car, it had taken Gerry almost half an hour to get his distraught wife to explain to him what had happened and to calm down. Then, after she had described the weird event, he explained that the most likely reason for her believing she was undergoing some kind of psychic intrusion. Could be related to the stories they had heard about the Manor being haunted and talking of seeing the phantom figures.

Also the stress of losing the children so suddenly, and the amount of sedatives she was taking combined with the occasional glass of wine may have confused her. Gerry then asked if she had been drinking at the time of the weird phenomenon.

Ava had to admit that, against the doctor's advice, she had been drinking a glass of wine at the time, but she could understand what Gerry was saying and reluctantly got out of the car. Ava did however, hang on to Gerry's arm when they entered the house where he gave her words of encouragement as he led her through the hallway and up the wide sweeping staircase. Then went onto the balcony and into the bathroom where he helped her out of her wet clothing and told her to take a hot shower.

At first, Ava had been hesitant, saying that if she did take a shower then he must stay in the bathroom with her. To appease her, Gerry sat on the bathroom chair until she was done, then waited in the bedroom until she had found something warm to wear. He next took Ava down the stairs and into the kitchen where he made her a hot drink in the hope of helping her relax.

His next words came as a shock to her when he insisted that she either stop taking the sedatives or stop drinking. It didn't take long for Ava to decide what was the most important, a clear head or an occasional glass of wine. The wine won and, in an effort to prove to Gerry that she was not addicted to the tablets, Ava emptied each bottle of pills down the kitchen sink.

He had to hide a smile though when she asked him to help her turn the heavy oak desk around so that it would be facing the door. This would enable her see anyone who was entering her office; she had also placed the chair near the wall so that no one could sneak up behind her.

The rest of the day and the night passed without incident and the following morning Ava was up bright and early. She had managed to pushed the previous day's events to the back of her mind and had got on with preparing breakfast. By seven-thirty, she had awoken Gerry and Sally by serving them breakfast in bed, and by the time Gerry came downstairs, he found Ava hard at work on the latest edition of the magazine face cover. Taking care not to alarm her, he tapped lightly on the open door while at the same time calling her name.

"Is it alright if I come in for a few minutes?" he asked coming to her side and kissing her cheek as he ruffled her hair. Ava responded by returning his kiss and smiled.

"I've already set up our evening meal so you can sort out lunch for us both, and if you decide to make a coffee for yourself then I will have one with you and a biscuit."

"It's good to see you're back on form and giving orders," he joked as he left the room.

Just then the phone rang, it was Betty Thomas one of their neighbours calling to say that she and her husband Phil would be delighted to come to the house-warming. She then asked if they needed any help with the preparations for the party.

"No," Ava replied, "but thank you for your kind offer of help. Gerry and I have arranged for the catering companies who have organised our previous parties to take care of the preparations."

"Mrs Wilson…"

"Oh please don't be so formal, call me Ava."

"Ava, would it inconvenience you if we brought along another couple, I know they aren't invited but they are dying to meet you."

Ava stopped her in mid-sentence. "Of course you can, and if anyone else wishes to bring another couple then it will be fine."

Ava felt a sense of pleasure sweep through her at Betty's response. Throughout the following days, they received numerous telephone calls from friends, relatives and neighbours accepting the invitations that Gerry had posted through doors and mailed out to friends and business associates.

Surprisingly, most of the invited guests asked if they could bring along friends and by mid-week Ava and Gerry realised that there must be about seventy or eighty guests on the list, along with Ava and Gerry's parents who would be arriving on the Friday to stay for a long weekend.

Chapter 17
Sally

That night an unanticipated problem arose just as Gerry and Ava were preparing for bed.

"Listen," Gerry whispered to Ava holding his finger to his lips. "Can you hear it?"

Ava nodded her head and took hold of Gerry's hand when hearing the sound of sobbing as someone slowly walked past their bedroom door and along the balcony.

"Oh God, what now?" Ava quivered reaching for her dressing gown and pulling it around herself.

"Stay where you are while I go find out." Gerry donned his dressing gown and opened the bedroom door with Ava close behind. "I told you to stay here, now get back to bed."

"I can't; I'm too scared to be on my own," she whispered urgently. "I'm coming with you."

"Oh for goodness sake," he muttered cursing under his breath. "Don't switch on any lights; if it's an intruder we don't want them to be aware that we've heard them," he hissed. "If it's a ghost, oh shit," he shuddered at the thought.

Unknown to Ava, Gerry was just as scared as she was and grabbed hold of the ornamental silver candle holder standing in the centre of the table to use as a weapon.

In the darkness, Gerry silently groped his way along the balcony as he followed the heart-breaking sobs until reaching the staircase leading to the attic, where he stopped and flicked on the light switch.

"Oh my God" he cried, when seeing his daughter Sally in the sudden bright light, sobbing and frantically clawing at the locked attic door. She was oblivious to the pain from the cuts on her bloodstained fingers and broken nails, nor the freezing cold air surrounding her in her unwavering effort to get into the attic.

Gerry lost no time in grabbing hold of his daughter and carrying her down the staircase and into her bedroom and laid her on the floral duvet, where Ava gently awoke her telling her that everything was alright. But as soon as Sally saw her blood-stained night dress and bleeding fingers, she became hysterical and began screaming.

"Mummy, Mummy, I had this terrible dream," she sobbed. "I was being murdered! I tried to escape but the man who laid on top of me was suffocating me."

"Darling, you're safe now; it was only a bad nightmare," Ava said hugging her terrified daughter and turned to her husband who was anxiously watching, not knowing what to do.

"Gerry, could you get the antiseptic from the medicine chest in the kitchen cupboard while I take her into the bathroom to clean her hands and change her night clothes."

Gerry nodded and hurried down stairs to the kitchen, but drew to a sudden halt when seeing the dark shadow of a man lurking near the open doorway.

"What the hell." Gerry's nerves were already on edge, and at that precise moment, Gerry was so hyped he was ready to kill to protect his family, and he stood his ground.

"I don't know who the hell you are," he shouted, "but you had better get out of here right now or I will beat the fucking daylights out of you."

Gerry's fists were clenched and his face was almost purple with rage as he took a menacing step towards the loitering figure. To Gerry's surprise, the man appeared to dissolve in front of him.

"Oh shit," he moaned when realising what it was. He didn't have the time though to let himself be upset by the sight of a ghost; nevertheless, he did wonder if it had had anything to do with Sally's strange behaviour.

"Where's the fucking antiseptic?" he snarled pulling everything out of the cupboard and throwing it onto the unit top until he found the medicine box. Then stared at its contents not knowing which article to take upstairs.

"Bugger it, I'll take the lot," he muttered sweeping everything back into the box and hurried upstairs to his daughter's room where he handed Ava the medical kit.

By now, she had managed to calm Sally, but Sally was still shaky from her nightmare and crying.

"Gerry," she whispered to her husband who was now seated on a chair beside the bed and holding Sally's hand while Ava applied soothing cream and ointment to her damaged fingers. "I think we should give her one of the sedatives that the Mr Daniels told us to give her in case she should walk in her sleep, and I'll stay the night with her just in case."

Gerry agreed.

"You're right. Tomorrow," he said, "we will make an appointment for her to see Mr Daniels and explain to him what has happened. This is the third time this has occurred since she came home, and she can't go on like this, otherwise she is going to really hurt herself if we're not careful."

"Can you get a glass of water then she can take the tablet."

Gerry nodded and went into the bathroom and filled the glass then returned to Ava, who promptly took the glass and held it while Sally swallowed the pill.

After waiting for the drug to take effect, Sally became calm and slid down beneath the sheets, and after tucking the bedding around Sally, Ava turned on the night light and climbed into the bed opposite, as Gerry left the room closing the door softly behind him.

Chapter 18
Sally Part 2

Mr Daniels agreed to see Sally straight away when Gerry rang for an appointment, and they were shown into his private rooms as soon as they arrived. The first question he asked if Sally was experiencing somnambulism while at school. Ava told him that she had rang St Elizabeth's and spoken to Miss Brocklehurst. In reply, Miss Brocklehurst had informed Ava that Sally who shared a dorm with her friend Hilary always slept peacefully every night.

Mr Daniels then proceeded to ask Sally if anything at home or at school was troubling her, she had replied no. Then after he had examined her thoroughly Mr Daniels informed Ava and Gerry that he could find nothing mentally nor physically wrong with Sally. He did however, believe that the problem may be psychological, and suggested that at a later date they could try hypnosis.

Gerry baulked at the idea and immediately declined, saying that Sally had suffered enough without having to remember the ugly, unpleasant memories of her brothers' and her aunt Caroline's gruesome deaths being brought to the surface. He only wished that he himself could forget the carnage he had seen that day.

Mr Daniels nodded his head sympathetically, as he understood what Gerry was saying. But he did find it rather odd though, that Sally should start walking in her sleep as soon as she returned to the Grange. Therefore, he suggested that the problem perhaps could be related to something in the house that was disturbing her. He advised them, that while Sally was at home they should keep a watchful eye on her, especially at night, and make sure that every window and door be locked. Also, to make certain that she took the prescribed medication while she was at home.

"Can we go for a walk, Daddy?" Sally asked as soon as they arrived home.

"Of course we can, sweetheart, but first we have to get changed and put warmer clothing on and our boots, we're not dressed for this weather, are we?" he said glancing up at the snow-filled sky. "We've got to be prepared, haven't we?"

Sally followed his gaze up into the sky, "I think you're right, we do have to be prepared for the worst, don't we?"

Sally's words sent a shudder of fear through Gerry, what did she mean for the worse he questioned silently. Was she aware of something that he didn't know of. Shit, I'm becoming paranoid' he muttered to himself.

He then recalled the conversation with Miss Brocklehurst shortly after Sally had returned to school.

She had informed him that Sally was surpassing all other students in her classes, and they were considering taking her to a higher level of education where she would be among students of equal learning. But more disturbing was the fact that she was accurately prophesising some of the other students' future. This she had been ordered to stop doing immediately, otherwise she would be expelled from the school This had surprised both Ava and Gerry, as Sally had never shown any sign of being academic, nor being psychic. Otherwise, she would have been aware of the preceding accident and would have warned Caroline not to make the perilous journey.

They were also surprised by Sally's response when they had asked her what gifts she would like for Christmas. To their amazement she didn't want any of the articles that a girl of her age wanted, instead she had asked for books of psychology, biology, pathology and Mathematics and nothing more. Then to add to their confusion, throughout the holiday she taken to walking around the estate with her father and pointing out various plants, weeds, and bushes and explaining their potential therapeutic remedies.

Building snowmen and the snowball fights that Gerry used to have with all three children were a thing of the past, Sally had told him that she didn't have the time to play silly childish games anymore. She preferred to stay in her room and study for the forthcoming exams at Easter.

What Ava found disturbing was that Sally would not let her go into her study where she did her school work and kept her books.

Nevertheless, one day Ava took the opportunity to look inside Sally's room while she was outside walking with her father. She was surprised to see that everything was aligned in perfect order and her bedroom was tidy. This was so unlike Sally, as in the past her clothing and toys would have been strewn untidily about the room, and Ava would have stifled a laugh when Sally would appear, smiling from ear to ear, with cosmetic make-up smeared all over her face.

Ever since the accident however, those days were now gone, their daughter had changed and at nights Sally would wake from horrific nightmares and sit up in bed screaming.

When this happened, Ava would comfort and calm her until she fell asleep again, but it was the somnambulism that concerned Ava most of all.

At times, she would be awoken by Sally, who was fast asleep, tugging at the bedroom door screaming that she had to escape from the bedroom.

It was a relief however, for Ava and Gerry when it came to the time for Sally to return to St Elizabeth's.

The first thing Sally did was to carefully pack her new books into a strong carton so they wouldn't be damaged on her journey back to school, then her clothing was neatly folded and packed into a holdall.

But when the transport arrived to take her back to St Elizabeth's, Sally distressed her parents by giving them an emotionless farewell. Also, she didn't turn towards the window and wave goodbye to them as she left; she just sat staring straight ahead and totally ignored them as they stood waving tearfully to the rear of the vehicle as it drove away from The Grange.

Chapter 19
Strange Happenings

The following week was hectic, and Gerry had to go to London for three days to take care of business that couldn't be done from his office at home. Ava travelled to Liverpool and stayed over for a number of days to discuss an important new feature that could be added to the magazine.

Ava and Gerry could hardly believe how quickly the time had flown due to their busy work schedules, and by the time Friday was upon them both sets of in-laws had arrived that morning, Gerry's from Devon, and Ava's from Yorkshire and were already upstairs unpacking.

By coincidence, they had booked into the same hotel the previous evening and had decided to travel to North Yorkshire together.

By two o' clock, the Grange was agog with activity, and Ava had decided that they would have to use the ballroom for the number of guests they were expecting. The extra low tables that she had hired for the occasion were already set in place in front of the chaise longue, sofas, and well sprung chairs placed on either side of the ballroom floor. The ornate banqueting table that had been left behind by the previous owners was opened out to its full capacity.

The caterers had already laid the tables with frilly tablecloths, with wine and champagne glasses, and placed alongside these were glasses for men who preferred beer. Porcelain plates and silver cutlery were set aside for the main meal, and side plates for sandwiches and hors d'oeuvres. Nearby, were floral design cut glass dishes for desserts that completed the lavish settings, and napkins for the messy eaters were placed about the tables.

Meanwhile, both Gerry's and Ava's parents, who had arrived early, were happy with the rooms they had been given, although Ava at first had baulked at the idea of giving them the boys' bedrooms. Gerry however had done his best to explain to Ava that the rooms would only be standing empty and it was best if they were used. It almost broke his heart when moving the boys' treasured belongings into one of the empty rooms upstairs.

On the Saturday morning, Gerry's father, Michael, had taken Gerry to one side and commented that it was rather a peculiar if not a strange house.

When Gerry asked what he meant, Michael told Gerry that his mother was afraid. She'd told him that when she had walked down the corridor to the kitchen to help Ava prepare breakfast, she had sensed someone walking behind her, but when she turned to see who it was, no one was there.

Helen had been so scared that she ran to the kitchen to be near Ava.

There was also another incident he said, when Helen had left the bedroom that morning to come down stairs, she had noticed a woman dressed in a blue gown watching her from the balcony above.

To be honest, he said, the place was giving her the creeps, and even though the daylight was poor that morning due to the fog and falling snow, Michael, told Gerry, that he had noticed the weird shape of a man standing opposite their bedroom door who appeared to merge into the wall when he approached him. Not only that but they had also sensed another person in the bedroom with them last night, yet when he turned on the bedside lamp, no-one was there.

"To be honest, son, your mother and I don't like this house," he added sternly. "It is too big and we think you should move out now that the boys are gone."

"Can you turn the light on? It's getting dark in here?" Michael asked when the daylight unexpectedly began to fade.

Gerry switched on the light and turned to face his father. "Please Dad, don't say anymore, especially not when Ava is within hearing distance when referring to the boys. She's having a hard time getting accustomed to them not being here, and the slightest wrong word could send her back into the depression that she's been fighting hard to overcome. She is still trying to come to terms with what happened to the boys, and to Caroline."

His father gave him an understanding look as he placed a comforting hand on his shoulder.

"I'm sorry son, I wasn't thinking, I understand, and I won't say another word about the boys, but you've got to remember; your mother and I have lost our daughter as well as our two grandchildren."

Michael paused for a moment shaking his head. "I don't know how you and Ava can drive up and down that road where it happened."

He fell silent when the lights began flickering on and off.

"What's wrong with the lights, do they—?" Michael broke off what he was about to say, when hearing the sound of heavy booted footsteps heading towards the cellar. "What the hell's that?"

"I don't know," Gerry replied, moving towards the open door.

"Did you see anything?"

"No, and it wasn't my imagination either, but something or somebody has just walked past us."

Gerry broke into a sweat. "You don't think it could have been a—?"

"Shush, listen," Michael whispered. "Somebody is in one of the front rooms."

"They can't be; Ava and Helen are in the kitchen, and Frank and Elsie are still in bed upstairs."

They stared at one another in silence, then stiffened, when hearing the unexpected sound of heavy furniture being moved about as if it were on bare wooden floorboards in the room ahead of them.

"Oh shit, you're right; somebody is in there, but the floor it's carpeted so—"

"Shush," Michael whispered holding his fingers to his lips, then walked over to the room and stood listening for a few moments before flinging the door wide open. To their amazement, they saw that all of the furniture had been rearranged.

"What the hell," Gerry stared about the room in shock by what he was seeing. "I can't believe it, there was nobody in here, and it would have taken three or four men to lift that sideboard," he uttered, gaping incredulously at the high, three-sectioned piece of oak furniture that was now placed against the wall opposite the bay window.

"I need a drink," Michael mumbled, pushing Gerry out of the room towards his office. "I told you I didn't like this place, it's too big and not only that, there's a lot of bad history going with it, and it's reputed to be haunted by God only knows what. And while I'm at it, if you're staying, why don't you change the decoration and brighten the place up a bit. For goodness sake, a normal house doesn't have so many long, dingy, dark corridors separating every room that you have to go through to get to another room. It's like a bloody maze trying to find your way around the place. And another thing; why does the attic have to be kept under lock and key? Bloody hell, it's like a fucking mausoleum." He yelled in frustration.

"Dad, I told you when we first came here," Gerry felt his temper rising as his voice threatened to reach breaking point, "this house is a Grade 1 listed building and we cannot, nor do we want to, change anything here. Ava and I love the decoration and the period furniture that Jack brought in for us. It fits in with the surroundings, it is part of the building's heritage."

"Huh," Michael gave a disgruntled grunt, "I suppose you will be telling me next, ghosts included."

"Dad," Gerry groaned in frustration, "can we move away from here before something else happens?" he suggested, guiding his father into his spacious office, where he stopped to peer warily about the room before entering, to seat themselves in the comfortable armchairs.

"I don't understand it, nothing like this has happened before," Gerry's voice held a nervous edge as he spoke.

"First time for me as well," his father replied. "I told you I didn't like the bloody place and I think you should leave before something else bad happens."

"Dad, give me a break, for goodness sake, we've only just moved in. Maybe what happened to Caroline and the boys was just a one-off." Gerry wasn't convinced by what he was saying when hearing the worried tone in his own voice.

Just then, he heard Ava calling to him from the kitchen.

"I've got to go," Gerry walked over to the door and left the room. "What is it?" he asked when reaching the kitchen and opening the door. To his surprise the kitchen was empty. "Ava, Helen," he called.

"What?" Ava replied from the from the upstairs balcony.

Gerry moved out of the kitchen and was surprised to see Ava standing on the first floor landing. Forcing himself to stay calm, he said, "My mistake I thought I heard you calling to me from the kitchen."

"No, I've been showing Elsie and Frank around upstairs for the last half hour."

Gerry felt his skin crawl as both he and Michael had heard her call his name from the kitchen.

"Okay, no problem, it must have been the birds I heard outside," he replied turning to face Michael who had followed him and was standing directly behind him.

"I don't like this," Michael muttered, taking hold of Gerry's arm and leading him back into the office. "I don't like this at all, we both heard Ava calling your name from the kitchen." Michael glanced nervously into the shadowed areas of the hall. "It's as if something is trying to separate us. Gerry, I need to get some fresh air to clear my head; why don't you come with me, we both need—"

"Dad, please," Gerry interrupted him.

But his father was desperate to get away from the building.

"I'm not staying in here and that's final. Now if you don't mind, I'll go for a walk and take a look around outside. Maybe I'll go see what's in those old buildings on the other side of the Hall."

"Fine by me," Gerry replied. "I can't leave Ava, my mother, Elsie and Frank alone in the house, not after what's just happened. But you'd better get well wrapped up because it's started snowing again and this time it's heavier than before."

"Have you been in those stone outbuildings, you know which ones I mean, they are on your land, aren't they?" his father asked.

"Yes, they are, but I haven't had the time to check them out yet," Gerry replied. "I don't even know if they're locked."

"Not to worry, I'll go take a look around and let you know if I find anything useful out there."

Michael went to the hall cupboard and donned his outdoor clothing. "See you later," he called as he left the manor.

Chapter 20
The Outbuildings

Michael held his head down low as the snow and icy wind whipped around him. At times, he almost fell when the strong blasts of wind threatened to bring him to his knees, as each powerful gust sent him staggering forward through the deep dunes of snow that were constantly whipped up by the force of the howling gale.

When driving up the road the previous day, he had noticed that there was a row of low stone buildings that he guessed must have stood roughly seven feet high, plus a slightly taller one at the end that would have been about nine feet. Each of them appeared to be derelict but he believed that if they were of a decent standard, then it wouldn't take much for them to be renovated and put to good use.

However, he could hardly make them out right now as his vision had become blurred due to the stinging icy flakes of snow. And he couldn't help but wonder if the weather had been like this on the fateful day when his daughter and grandchildren had died, and felt a sob rise in his throat.

Come on, you silly old fool, he thought to himself feeling each blast of cold air chill him to the bone. *You didn't come out here to depress yourself, you came outside to escape the bloody ghosts.*

Michael forced himself to concentrate on the stone buildings. At a guess, he gauged that the buildings were quit a distance away from the manor and would have been surrounded by the trees and bushes. But as the plants were now without foliage the buildings were clearly visible.

There were a few evergreens that partially concealed the old buildings from the Grange.

In the summer time though, the trees would have created a perfect camouflage for the manor and would have been hidden from the sight of the household and visitors' view, as they were quite a distance away and standing in a more open area from the manor.

The wind had blown the snow across the open tract of land and created deep snow drifts in certain parts of the terrain making it hard for Michael to find a firm footing. Nevertheless, regardless of the howling wind and the storm's rising magnitude, Michael's curiosity was aroused and he struggled on through the deep, undisturbed snow.

He was grateful to find that when he did finally manage to reach the double wooden doors, they were unlocked, and he pushed one of them open and entered.

Michael discovered that it was just as cold inside as it was out, but at least he was sheltered and away from the blustery snow storm. He was surprised to find that it was totally empty and had been swept clean apart from a few cobwebs, as well as mouse and rat droppings. The only sign of it ever having being used was where holes had been gouged into the walls where shelving had been fixed in the past. He presumed that the builder must have removed them.

Perplexed, Michael moved onto the next building where he found them in exactly the same condition. But when he entered the last stone building that was higher than the rest, he found it to be in a bedraggled state.

It was filthy, traces of undisturbed vermin were scattered about the floor, huge masses of cobwebs that hadn't been disturbed for years clung to his clothing and head when his body came into contact with them, and the smell of damp and decay was beginning to make him feel nauseous.

On glancing around, he noticed two antiquated four-wheeled carts with flaking paint that were parked together in the farthest corner of the building, these were stacked with mouldy empty wooden casks.

Rotting leather bridles hung from rusty fittings in the walls, saddles were strewn across solid wooden benches along with a mass of other objects, making it obvious that no one had been in there for years. Everywhere he turned, he saw items that were swathed and almost hidden beneath thick layers of dirt and cobweb.

In confusion, Michael stood shaking his head. Why were all of the other barns clean and this one left neglected and filthy with items that could have been sold for a profit years ago?

Unanswerable questions raced through his mind, but as Michael turned to leave, he felt his heart suddenly leap with fear, when he saw a man dart past him and race through the open door into the stormy weather outside.

"What the hell," he muttered, hurrying to the door, but he was too late; the man had gone.

Michael had noticed that the man was not wearing a coat and when he glanced down into the snow, he froze; there were no footprints denoting that anyone had ever been there.

"Oh shit," he murmured, pulling the heavy door closed behind him, then hurried back towards the house only to find his pale-faced wife waiting at the door.

"Thank God you're alright," she fussed helping him off with his hooded coat and woolly hat. "I was just about to send someone searching for you."

"Why? I told Gerry where I was going."

"That might be," she replied in a worried tone. "But a man came to the door and told us that you'd had an accident in one of the old buildings over there." She pointed in the direction from where he had just been. "Gerry has gone out searching for you."

Without another word, Michael pulled his hat and coat back on. "Don't open the door to anybody," he shouted as he stepped out into the howling wind.

Helen was just about to ask why, but was too late, Michael was already gone and retreating towards the outbuildings where he noticed that one of the large barn doors was gaping wide open.

"I closed that," he muttered, then braced himself as he cautiously entered the dark shadowy structure. "Oh my God," was all he could say when he found Gerry staring in awe at the apparition of young stable lad grooming a magnificent pure white Arabian stallion.

"I would never have believed this if I weren't seeing it for myself," he whispered huskily.

"What do we do?" Gerry asked not daring to take his gaze away from the phenomenal sight.

"I don't rightly know," Michael's voice quivered as he spoke, then grabbed hold of Gerry's arm as the apparitions slowly disappeared. "Come on, let's get out of here, and not a word to your mother," Michael whispered, locking eyes with his terrified son. "Do you hear me!" he shouted at Gerry to shake him out of his shocked state. "Not a word to your mother or anyone, do you understand?"

Gerry nodded his head; at that moment, he was too traumatised to say anything.

"Come on." Michael ushered his son out of the barn, then ensuring that the door was securely closed behind them, they headed back towards the Manor.

Thankfully, on their return they found the rest of the family in the lounge where the women were drinking coffee and Frank was sat with a glass of whisky in his hand.

"I wouldn't mind a whisky, do you want one, Dad, I'm frozen after being out there." Gerry threw a look of concern towards his father who was stood rubbing his cold hands together.

"I wouldn't mind a coffee as well," his dad replied, giving him a glance not to say anything as he seated himself on the sofa.

"I take the hint," Ava retorted testily as she got up and went into the kitchen to prepare a fresh pot for the two men.

When she returned with the coffee, she found everyone sat around talking about the coming party, and Gerry and Michael with a tumbler each filled to the brim with whisky, plus a fresh unopened bottle in front of them.

In an instant, she knew that something bad must have occurred while they were outside, but had the sense not to ask what it was.

Chapter 21
The Party

Saturday morning was hectic; the caterers had delivered the food by three o' clock, and the doors dividing the ballroom had been opened wide, turning it into one large room for the expected guests. One of the tables contained glasses for wine and shorts, another cutlery, plates and napkins.

The plates filled with various cakes were wrapped in cellophane and the large banqueting table was set and ready to be filled with a selection of cooked sliced meats, fish, coleslaw, potato salad and various dishes and dressings plus the hors-d'oeuvres that needed to be kept in the fridges.

For entertainment, they had hired a DJ for ten pm, so if any one wished to dance, they could let their hair down and enjoy themselves.

Gerry welcomed their neighbours who were the first to arrive followed by both his friends and Ava's. Once they were assembled in the ballroom, they were handed drinks of their choice, and within no time at all, the Grange was abounding and buzzing with life.

"I like your idea of a butler showing us through to the banquet," Maria said, gazing about in open admiration of the elegant surroundings.

"Yes, we found it very stylish and in keeping with the past of the old manor," Gina chorused along with more of the guests.

Ava threw Michael a puzzled glance who shook his head and put a finger to his lips. He later took her to one side asking if she had hired anyone to greet the guests.

Before she had the chance to reply, they overheard one of the women quoting what a quaint costume the butler was wearing.

"Yes, that powdered wig with the ponytail."

"Don't forget those white breeches and black jacket," Maria added with a giggle.

"He certainly showed his manhood in those tight pants."

"He certainly did," another replied.

"Well, I wouldn't kick him out of bed, like I do with Bernard every morning," she threw a contemptuous glance over at her husband who was beginning to form a middle-age spread.

They all laughed as they glanced at the men who were stood talking with drinks in their hands.

"If anyone would like to eat, there's plenty of food, so don't be shy everybody, come and get it," Frank announced with a laugh over the intercom system. "I want all of the food eaten before you go home," he jovially told them. "It's free, so come on everyone tuck in, and fill your glasses."

The wine waitress went around filling empty glasses, while the others served the food.

A number of men stood about in groups talking and drinking, while other guests seated themselves with plates of food and drink on the luxurious furniture spread about the spacious room, introducing themselves and chatting to one another.

"Who do you think that woman was who went upstairs in the beautiful blue evening gown?" Maria asked a group who had clustered together. "She looked absolutely stunning."

"I saw her walking down the hall, she must have been lost," another replied.

"Well, I've never seen her before," Gina added haughtily giving a flippant smirk. "She's not from around here or I would have recognised her, but she did appear to know her way about the Grange and she went into the front room, that one over there," she said, pointing towards the closed door.

"Do you think she was meeting someone in there on the quiet?"

"Have you been snooping again?" Jean giggled, feeling herself becoming slightly tipsy from drinking too much wine.

Just then Ava came towards them asking if they would like a tour of the house.

"All of the other ladies have agreed to come."

"Yes, please," they chorused, eager to find out what was in the upstairs rooms.

"Well, whenever you are ready; the ladies are waiting at the bottom of the staircase."

Before they started the tour, Ava pointed out that the parts of the West Wing of the mansion that had not been completely destroyed the fire had been sealed off.

She then explained that as the building was classed as a Grade 1 structure, then the remaining damaged section of the ruins that were still safely standing could be rebuilt at some time.

Therefore, when a grant became available, The National Heritage Society, who had been interested in purchasing the Old Hall previously, would restore it to its original condition. It would become a paying tourist attraction especially with its past history of judicial malice, and the innocents being sent to the gallows.

"Oh no, you're not thinking of selling, are you? We don't want sightseers around here, do we, girls?" Betty asked angrily.

"No, we don't," they responded in unison.

"Why didn't they put in an offer to buy while it was empty?" Anna asked pointedly.

"I've no idea," Ava replied. "We must have made the estate agent a better offer. Now ladies, shall we begin the tour by starting downstairs. As you are aware, this was the ballroom but it can be turned into two rooms when the central doors are closed."

"What's in there?" Gina asked pointing to the room where the woman had entered.

"That's the television room, we don't use it very often as we're too busy, plus there isn't anything worth watching," she added with a smile.

They followed her through the maze of passages until reaching the two central rooms, one of which she pointed out, would have been the games room for the gentlemen. This was arranged with two long slate billiard tables with huge brass lights suspended overhead from the ceiling by thick brass chains. The cues and rests were placed in a specially designed frame, and a mahogany counter board was set in the wall to keep the score. Alongside these antique artefacts were dart boards, a roulette table, and numerous card and games tables, and a fully equipped bar. Plush seating surrounded the entire room, with low tables for when the men rested for a while.

The second room was mainly for the ladies who liked an occasional game of cards, they most likely did their gossiping in here where it was private, along with their knitting, crocheting. Ava pointed to the antique boxes standing on their finely carved legs.

"These still contain silver scissors, thimbles, needles and cotton threading aids, every tool that was necessary for their needlepoint and tapestry work. Some of the other boxes contain a variety of sizes of bone and silver knitting needles," she added opening the lids for them to see what was inside. "As you can see, there is both a harpsicord and a grand piano over by the window that is overlooking the rose gardens. If you look through the windows, you will see to the rear of the property, on either of these rooms, there is a solid high wall. That is all that was left standing after the fire devastated the main section of the building that collapsed into the cellar."

"You will notice however, that there are two empty large areas on either side of these two rooms. Mr Armstrong, the builder, assumed that each one could have been used as an orangery where the occupiers would catch the sunlight at various hours of the day."

"They would also have been used as somewhere for the ladies to sit during the summer time, and keep away from the harmful rays of the sun that would discolour their delicate white skin."

"Mr Armstrong also kept the two stone pillars that were unaffected by the blaze he left them as extra support for the rooms above at either end of the property. He has also built a low stone wall surrounding the open rooms, and as you can see, he filled in the rest of the space with double glazed units."

She waited for them to gaze about the area and talk amongst themselves as they marvelled at the fine decorations and the amount of space of the Manor before moving forward. Ava then led them up the wide carpeted staircase and onto the balcony leading in two opposite directions, pointing out that there were eight bedrooms—four on either side with long corridors leading to each room; four at the front of the house and four at the rear. She explained that each bedroom had its own en-suite and walk-in wardrobe, plus there were two more centrally placed rooms at the rear of the back bedrooms.

Filled with curiosity, one of the women asked, "Can we see them?"

"Of course," Ava replied and escorted them to view each room.

After the viewing, Ava directed the group along the spacious corridor until reaching the corridor leading to the two centrally placed bedrooms. Once inside, they shuddered and gasped when a sudden blast of cold air spread over them when Ava opened the door onto a large spacious balcony.

"As you can guess, these spaces were built over the orangery so I suppose this must have been where the men sat talking and smoking when it was warm enough to do so. It is a bit chilly here, isn't it," she said with a smile and closed the door.

"Why would anybody in their right mind want to live in a house this size?" Brenda whispered to Sarah, who shrugged non-committally.

"What's through here?" Judy asked when reaching another door.

"Oh, that is a staircase leading to the attic," Ava replied. "We never go up there, anyway the door to the attic is double locked and we can't get through."

"But only a moment ago, I saw someone go up there?" Anna stammered in a confused manner, pointing to the door.

"Yes, I did too," Ella remarked, backing Anna's comments.

"What?" Ave responded in surprise. She opened the door to look up the steep twisting staircase to find out who had gone up, but no one was there.

"I think I had better go and check that door," she said to the women who were now mumbling among themselves and were becoming nervous and edgy. Putting on a brave face, Ava warily climbed the stairs until reaching the door and tried opening it but it was firmly locked.

"There, I told you it was locked, you must have been mistaken," she said when returning. "You can go up if you like and try opening it," she said to the nearest woman.

Betty offered to go and hesitantly climbed the twisting staircase until reaching the room and tried opening the door. But the handle wouldn't turn and she returned shaking her head.

This however, caused a great deal of confusion to both women who had seen a woman go up the staircase.

"She can't have just disappeared," Anna said glancing wildly about at the group of anxious faces watching her. "I didn't make it up! I swear! I did see her honestly."

"She could have if she was a ghost," Sarah whispered shakily.

"Oh God, let's get back to the others," Anna's voice echoed through the anxious silence that had fallen around them.

For a moment, no one moved until one woman turned tail and ran, hastily followed by the rest of them to where the men were now in the games room, talking politics and sport, while the others were playing billiards.

Chapter 22
Panic

"What the hell's wrong?" Derek asked in surprise at the sight of the white-faced women as they barged into the games room.

"Two of us have just seen a ghost going up into the attic," Anna blurted out loud enough for everyone to hear.

"And one going into the TV room," Gina added.

"What? You've all had too much to drink," Brian said, nudging Phil and laughing as he picked up the snooker cue and potted the green ball.

"Don't you dare make fun of us," Maria snapped moving forward and reached up to slap her husband's head.

"Hey, cut it out!"

"No, you listen to what we are saying, there is a ghost in this house and we're scared, we want you men to go upstairs right now and see it for yourselves."

For a moment, the men hesitated and looked at one another, before Gerry spoke, "Alright you guys, the ladies have had their fun, so it's your turn now."

He put down his snooker cue and gave the men a meaningful look then turned and walked towards the door with a troupe of disgruntled men, whose games had been interrupted, following behind him.

Gerry guided the men along the extensive lengths of winding corridors, up and down the staircases and everywhere in the house, explaining everything in detail, as Ava had to their wives.

"I didn't know you had a dog," Mel commented when seeing a huge Irish wolfhound go bounding past them towards the staircase.

"We haven't," Gerry replied, looking around at Mel.

"Well, I've just seen it, look it's sat there waiting for us." Mel pointed to the top of the staircase.

"There's nothing there," Gerry responded sharply, "you must be seeing things."

"Sorry Gerry, but I can back up what Mel just said, I saw it go down the staircase," Phil added.

"Oh God," Gerry muttered to himself suppressing, a cold shudder that ran through him. "Alright, it must be lost and has come from a neighbouring farm," he added shakily.

"Well, it seems to know its way about the house, and so did the other," Ray interrupted.

"Has anyone else seen them?" he asked, trying to control the tremor in his voice.

The men shook their heads and began mumbling uneasily amongst themselves.

"I've seen enough," Mel suddenly announced. "I think we ought to get back downstairs and finish our game. What do you say, Jim?"

"He's right, come on, we're not as nosy as the women," Jim was about to say more but stopped when noticing a dark shadow float through the wall opposite to where they were standing.

"What's up?" Darren asked turning to see what he was staring at, then sensed a disquieting unease when feeling something cold place a hand on his arm.

There was no time for heroics, or trying to remain calm, as Darren politely told the others that he was scared and going downstairs and headed for the staircase. Within minutes, the rest of the men followed suit and were right behind him as they hastily retreated down the stairs and into the games room. Being brave men, they headed straight for the bar and poured themselves a hefty drink to steady their fragmented nerves.

"What on earth is going on?" Ava asked when entering the games room. "We all heard you go thundering past and wondered what you were up to."

"I think we should be leaving, Linda, I've got a big workload tomorrow," Darren spoke sharply to his wife.

"What the Dickens is wrong with you," she looked at him with surprise written all over her face.

"Calm down, Darren," Gerry told him, putting a restraining hand on his shoulder. "We've all had a lot to drink and we have been telling ghost stories before we went upstairs."

"You can't tell me that it was my imagination because we all saw it." Darren looked towards the others for support, but they turned away embarrassed by the way they had all panicked and run.

"Has something happened to upset you?" Ava whispered to Darren, so that the others couldn't hear what she was saying.

"Yes," he replied glancing towards the group who were chatting amongst themselves before dropping his head in an embarrassed silence.

Ava took hold of his hand. "It's alright, you can tell me, some of the ladies have already seen something upstairs."

Daren lifted his head. "They have?" he mumbled, embarrassed by his behaviour. "You're not just saying that to make it sound as if—"

"No, I'm not." Ava glanced towards the others who were huddled in groups talking among themselves.

"Mel and Phil saw two dogs, Irish wolfhounds to be exact, then Jim saw something float through the wall and something cold touched me, I yelled and that's when we all ran."

Just then Helen and Michael entered the games room asking them to come to the ballroom and join in the dancing, Frank and Elsie were already whirling around the floor.

"Come on everybody, let's not waste any more time talking, we are here to enjoy ourselves so let's have some fun."

Michael then ushered everyone out of the games room and into the ballroom. "You can dance with anyone you please," he shouted over the sound of the music.

Within minutes, everyone was on the floor dancing and laughing as they changed partners whenever the DJ instructed. And by the time the night was through, everyone was filled with food and drink and had pushed the weird events from their minds.

Michael and Helen, along with Frank and Elsie, had been worn out with all the festivities by midnight and had retired earlier, leaving the rest of them to drink and party at their leisure.

It was 3 am, after the last two guests had left, that Ava found herself staring around at the disarray in the ballroom. Empty glasses and plates with half-eaten food were left on the tables and window ledges, and streamers that couples had thrown over each other were draped across the tables and chairs.

"Oh my goodness," Ava exclaimed despondently. "Look at the mess, what is Vivian going to say when she sees all—"

"Don't worry about it, love, Vivian will clean it up and the caterers will help her sort it all out tomorrow," he then hesitated and laughed. "Or should I say today."

"It's a good thing that Vivian has a key to let herself in," Ava yawned. "Come on, let's get to bed; I'm shattered."

Chapter 23
Leave the Grange

By the time Ava and Gerry had risen, Vivian had cleaned the ballroom and the caterers had taken away all of the extra dishes, plates, cutlery and glasses. They had stored the leftover food in Ava's own containers and placed them in the fridge and the half empty bottles of wine had been placed in the fridge cooler.

But when they entered the sitting room, they were surprised to see both sets of in-laws seated drinking coffee and talking about the previous night's events.

"Ah Gerry," Michael rose from the chair and took Gerry's arm, despite the quizzical looks that passed between the rest of them. Michel excused them both and led Gerry into the kitchen. "I wanted to have a word with you in private, son."

Gerry knew he must be about to say something serious due to the severity of his father's attitude and braced himself for what was coming next.

"I want you to leave this house."

"What?"

"I said that I want you to leave this house."

"Dad, we've only just moved in and we're getting to know our neighbours. I know that you don't like it here and say that it's too big for just the three of us. But when we have guests like you and Mum staying over and Frank and Elsie, well the place becomes more homely, don't you think?"

"No, I don't, this house is evil, it was built with tainted money and corrupt business dealings, and look what happened in that building outside; that was no figment of imagination. For God's sake, son, wake up to reality and get the hell away from here."

Michael paused for a moment when seeing Gerry's lips tighten in defiance just like they did when he was a child.

"Not only that but," Michael hesitated, "I truly believe that what happened to Caroline and the children was no accident."

"Dad, don't do this, don't say anymore."

"Why not, the truth always hurts, you've said so yourself."

"Please Dad, you've said enough, I'm going back to the others."

Gerry rose from the chair and left the room, leaving his father filled with concern for what would happen next.

"I think we ought to be heading home," Michael suddenly announced to his wife when he entered the sitting room.

"But it's only ten-thirty," Helen responded sharply.

"Look at the sky, Helen, we're going to get more bad weather and we have a long way to go."

"There's no problem there," Ava replied smiling, "you can all stay for as long as you wish, you don't have to decide right now, besides there are lots of leftovers for us to get through so food is no problem."

Gerry glanced towards his father.

Michael gave a shrug, rolled his eyes and held up his hands in defeat.

"Why don't we all go into the games room and have a game of cards," Helen suggested. "I love playing cards."

"You love playing anything," Michael mumbled so that she couldn't hear.

"By the way," Frank commented openly, "that man with the horse and cart was making a dammed racket this morning."

"Yes, it was well after we had all gone to bed," Elsie sighed, giving an audible yawn.

"It must have been the farmer from up the lane, but what the hell was he doing outside the Grange at that time of the morning?" Gerry remarked, annoyed by the farmer's lack of consideration.

"He had no right to be here, that man is a bloody nuisance, and he doesn't even try to get on with anyone, not even the locals. We have complained to the police about him splattering our cars with manure that drops from his trailer, and just to spite us, he drives the tractor in the centre of the road so we can't overtake him and his filthy vehicle. But the police have their hands tied, they can't do anything about it, it is a rural area and he does have the right to use the road, plus he was here before we came, they say."

"Well, apart from him, everyone is getting on quite well with the shopkeepers and the people in the village," Ava broke in, "so we tend to ignore him when we see him as do many of the locals."

"That doesn't give him the right to be outside your home making a racket, at goodness only knows what time it is in the morning," Frank grumbled, staring out of the window at the snow-covered ground. "By the way, Gerry, can I have a word with you in private when you've got the time to spare?"

"I've got time now," Gerry acknowledged getting to his feet and going over to the door.

"Come on, we can talk in the TV room."

"I'll join you," Michael said, wanting to hear what Frank had to say to Gerry.

Once they were away from the chattering women and seated in the TV room, Frank began asking questions regarding the security of the property, and demanding explanations relating to what had occurred in the early hours of that morning.

"What are you suggesting, Frank?" Gerry began. "The security is good; we have cameras and alarms fitted all about the house inside and out, so what's the problem?"

"I will tell you the problem," Frank said with a grim look on his face. "The moon was shining brightly, therefore with the snow covering the ground the whole area was lit up, and guess what?"

"What?" Michael snapped, impatient to hear what Frank had to say.

"Although we could hear more than one horse and a cart of some sort being pulled about in the area below and men's voices shouting to one another, when we opened the window to see who was causing the din, we couldn't see anybody, but the noise still persisted."

"Could you have been dreaming?" Gerry suggested throwing a nervous glance towards Michael who was sat grim-faced and digesting every word spoken.

"What, the two of us? You must be joking. And you may or may not believe what I am going to say right now you," he said emphatically moving his gaze from one man to the other.

"But when we looked down onto the gardens, there were no footprints from the men nor hoofmarks from the horses. The snow was completely undisturbed, so explain that if you can."

After a brief silence, Michael rose to his feet and began pacing the room before stopping in front of Gerry. "Are you going to tell him or shall I?"

"Tell me what? What's going on here?" Frank asked.

"The house is haunted."

"I thought as much," Frank stammered.

Gerry rose to his feet and was about to deny what Michael was going to say, but Michael held up a restraining hand advising him to listen.

"Two women saw the figure of a woman go up the stairs leading to the attic who didn't come down again. Mel and Phil saw two Irish wolfhounds on the balcony that disappeared on the staircase, and Darren panicked when he felt something cold touch him."

He turned to Gerry. "You tell him about what we both saw in the building outside."

Gerry glowered at Michael knowing that he had to face up to the fact that the house and the outbuildings were haunted, and began relating what they had seen.

"Holy shit," Frank gasped. "Elsie and I are leaving pronto."

Frank got to his feet and left the room shouting for Elsie to come upstairs right away. Then after explaining to her the urgency for them leaving and her agreeing, they hastily packed their belongings and went downstairs to where the others were waiting in the hall.

"Mum, Dad, you don't have to leave, please stay," Ava begged taking hold of her mother's hand.

"Ava, if you have an ounce of sense in your head then you will leave with us."

"But Mum, I can't, this is our home."

"That may be so, but your father and I think you should leave before something else bad happens," Elsie added tearfully.

"What do you mean something else bad," Michael snapped, annoyed by what was she was implying.

"You know dammed well what she means," Frank snarled.

Before anyone could say anything more, Frank had picked up their bags and ushered Elsie out into the garage, then got into the car and without a backward glance drove away.

Ava was stunned by the suddenness of their departure and broke down in tears, while Gerry, Helen and Michael stared after the car as it quickly disappeared into the vast curtain of snow that was falling more heavily than before.

"What do we do now?" Helen asked, nervously glancing about the hall and open staircase.

"Like I said earlier, I think we should be leaving before the snow blocks the road. You can see that it gets pretty bad out here so come on, let's get moving."

Helen reluctantly followed Michael up the stairs and into their room where she found that he had already packed and was ready to leave.

Without uttering another word, Helen and Michael gave Ava a hug and Gerry a firm handshake, before leaving them both standing tearfully in the doorway waving goodbye.

Chapter 24
The Introduction

After everyone had left, an unusual silence slowly descended into the house.

"What do we do now?" Ava asked tearfully.

"I don't know, let's have a cuppa and talk, although I don't know what the hell to talk about," Gerry said, rubbing his brow. "Do you want a hand?"

"No, I'm fine, I can manage."

"I'll be working in the office, give me a shout when it's ready and I'll carry it through to the TV room."

Ava went into the kitchen to brew fresh coffee for them both and set out a plate of sandwiches that she had taken from the fridge, along with two cups, cream and sugar and placed them on a tray.

But when she turned to place the coffee on the tray, Ava felt a surge of alarm when seeing that the tray had been moved and it was now set on the unit at the opposite side of the kitchen.

"Gerry! Gerry!" She screamed. Alarmed, Gerry came running from his office to see what was wrong.

"The tray," she said, pointing a quivering finger to the tray on the unit opposite.

"What's wrong with it?" he asked.

"I didn't put it over there, I put it on the unit here beside me."

"Don't worry about it, I'll stay here with you," he said, glancing nervously about the kitchen. "When it's ready, I'll carry it through into the lounge."

Ava's hand trembled as she picked up the coffee and placed it onto the tray, then watched as Gerry picked it up and carried it through into the lounge with Ava following close behind.

"Do you think the house is too big for us now that the boys are gone?" Gerry asked hesitantly. "Dad thinks it is."

"For once, I think your father is right," she replied gazing around at the massive high-ceilinged room. "The heating for one thing, you never know which way the economy is going to turn."

"Jack Armstrong said that we needn't worry about the cost of the heating for now," Gerry interrupted. "He had the coal and log bunkers filled to their capacity in the cellar before we arrived, and you know how big they are. They're from the original Hall and stand nearly as high as the cellar itself. They must be about…hmm…" He gazed thoughtfully into the fire. "I should roughly guess about fifteen-foot square, could be more."

"Gerry…"

"What?" he replied.

"Do you remember when Sally was home at Christmas?" Ava sat waiting for a reaction from him. "Well, do you?" she spoke sharply when he didn't answer immediately.

"Of course I do," he replied. "She never stopped talking about the new friends she'd made at St Elizabeth's, she was even planning to invite one of them home for the next Easter holiday."

"Yes, I know that, but didn't you think she was acting rather oddly, especially when she developed an obsession with the attic?"

"The attic?"

"Yes, the attic," she snapped impatiently at him.

"Come to think of it, I did," he murmured, rubbing his forehead thoughtfully. "That was when she was sleepwalking and we had to drag her downstairs away from the attic door."

"Yes, and what was she screaming?" Ava asked.

"Something about a chest, I can't remember, can you? I was too concerned about the damage she was doing to her hands than listening to what she was ranting and raving about. Oh no, somebody's at the door," he grumbled when the doorbell began ringing incessantly.

"Alright, alright," he shouted, "I'm coming." Gerry hurried to reach the door but when he opened it, he was surprised at seeing a man standing on his doorstep that he didn't recognise.

"Can I help you?" he asked.

"I would say that I can help you," the man replied staring intently at Gerry.

"Look, whatever you're selling, I don't want it."

"I'm not selling anything; what I have to say is about this house. Could I come in for a few moments to explain?" he asked giving a shudder. "It's freezing out here."

"Sorry." Gerry was about to close the door when the man put his foot inside, stopping him from doing so.

"Hey, that's enough!" Gerry's temper exploded, and he moved forward and pushed the stranger away, slamming the door in his face.

Ave had heard the raised voices and hurried into the hall where she found Gerry standing with fists clenched and his eyes filled with fury.

"What was all that about?" Ava asked in concern.

"I don't bloody know, it's some sodding stupid crank saying that he's come here to help us. For shits sake, he said it was about the house. Come on, let's get back inside, I'm freezing after standing at the door." He rubbed his cold hands together as they made their way back into the warmth of the room.

"Gerry," Ava suddenly asked, "how did he manage to get through the electric gates, I thought they were closed?"

Gerry gave a puzzled frown. "They were, I closed them after Dad left."

All of a sudden, Ava gave a scream and pointed when seeing the face of a man peering in at them through the window.

"What the bloody hell! It's him! That's the bloke who was at the door. That's it, I'll sort the bugger out now."

"Gerry, don't go outside," she cried grabbing hold of his arm to prevent him from leaving. "You never know, he could be dangerous; let me call the police."

Gerry hesitated, thinking for once Ava may be right, the man could be dangerous. He decided not to go outside and confront him. "Alright," he said, "you call the police, while I close the curtains."

Gerry released the cord allowing the heavy silken drapes to swing across the window while Ava rang the police.

Within minutes, the police had arrived and the man was arrested and placed in the police car while another officer, Sergeant Hill, came inside to speak with Ava and Gerry.

"We have questioned him, Sir, and he is adamant that he has come to help you, he claims to be a clairvoyant."

"Oh shit, that's all we need right now, a fucking headcase."

"If you don't mind me saying, Sir," Sergeant Hill continued, "he is well known in the village." He smiled, "My wife goes regularly to the meetings at the village hall to hear him speak as do most of the locals, he is pretty good if you don't mind me saying so."

"Well, life can get pretty dull and boring out here," Gerry said in a sardonic tone, "especially when you've got nothing better to do with your time."

"As you say, sir. But would it be alright with you if we just gave him a warning this time and tell him not to bother you again and to stay away from your property? Otherwise, he will be arrested for committing a stalking offence."

The conversation was suddenly interrupted when Ava gave a sharp gasp and leapt to her feet, and pointing to the open doorway. Immediately, everyone's attention was taken to where Ava was staring and saw in a shimmering halo of light, the figure of a sad-faced beautiful young woman holding out her left hand that she slowly lifted, and pointed upwards towards the balcony then slowly dissolved within a pale silver light.

"Oh my god, that chap was right, there is something here," Hill garbled as the apparition slowly faded in front of them. "I'd never have believed it if I hadn't seen it for myself," he quivered.

"I don't care who he is; bring the man in!" Ava yelled. "I want him in here now."

Gerry didn't argue, because he was still in shock from what he had just seen. "Go get him," he shouted at Hill who was rooted to the spot in fright. "I said go get him now."

The sound of Gerry's thundering voice pulled the Sergeant out of the trance.

"Go," Gerry pointed to the door.

"Yes, Sir," the Sergeant stammered and raced outside to the waiting police car.

Within minutes, the man was in the entrance hall introducing himself, while Hill stood waiting nervously by the door.

"Hello, I'm Alex Johnson," the man said holding out his hand. "I've come to help you."

Chapter 25
The Unexpected Guest

Gerry didn't take the man's proffered hand; instead, after taking one look at Alex's bedraggled appearance, Gerry demanded that he removed his dripping wet coat and muddy boots before moving any further into the house.

It was obvious, as soon as Alex had removed his wet clothing, that he looked after himself. His rugged five feet eleven-inch stance, untidy mop of long brown wavy hair and rugged tough looks gave the impression that he was used to living a basic lifestyle.

"Okay, what now?" he asked as Gerry stood watching and weighing him up.

"Come on, follow me," Gerry said begrudgingly.

Gerry led Alex into the lounge where Ava was stood waiting nervously and introduced Alex to her. She was surprised by his firm hand grip, but most of all she felt a fleeting sense of recognition when looking into his piercing blue eyes.

For some obscure reason, she felt as though he knew her, but more worrying was sensing that he was scanning her mind.

The fleeting sensation was broken by Sergeant Hill, asking Gerry if he wanted Alex to stay, or if he should take him away with them.

"No," Ava responded sharply.

In the short space of time they were stood talking, Ava had noticed the anxiety in Sergeant Hill's eyes as he glanced nervously about the room, and saw that he was uncomfortable and nervous by being at the Grange.

"You can go," she said with a dismissive gesture to the Sergeant, "but I want him to stay and explain what he means about us needing help."

Alex threw Ava a smile of gratitude while Gerry stood frowning until finally giving in, and agreeing for Alex to stay.

Sergeant Hill, then turned towards Alex and warned him, that as they were aware of him being inside the Grange, then they would be waiting outside the gates for a couple of hours in case of trouble. Also not to do anything he would regret later, or he would find himself under arrest.

Alex nodded, promising that he would not cause any problems for the couple, he was only there to help, and if at any time they wished him to leave then he would leave. Satisfied after hearing this Sergeant Hill left the Grange.

After the police were gone, Ava told Alex to sit down and wait while she went to get something for his feet and returned handing him a pair of warm sheepskin slippers that he gratefully slid onto his freezing cold feet. Gerry had made a fresh pot of coffee and placed it on the morning table along with a plate of biscuits.

As they drank the coffee, Gerry asked Alex. "How did you get here? We are miles from anywhere and it's knee deep in snow outside, so you can't have walked."

"I have a diesel four-wheel pickup parked up outside your property, I stood on the back and climbed over the wall. I was hoping to wait until it got dark—"

"Then you were going to break in and steal whatever you could carry," Gerry interrupted.

"No," Alex snapped angrily, rising to his feet and taking a step towards Gerry. "I was going to wait until dark then try to get some proof of the apparitions that have reportedly been seen around here. But if you're going to take that attitude then I'm going."

"Huh," Gerry snorted. "Do you expect me to believe that? Why did you look in through the window? Were you hoping that we would be out then you could break in and take your time rifling through everything?"

"That's enough, Gerry!" Ava shouted jumping to her feet and standing between the two men. "Alex said he was here to help us and I believe him. Now will you shut up and stop accusing him of doing something that he hasn't done, and sit down," Ava snapped sharply. "And you, Alex, sit down," she commanded sharply.

Alex gave her a look of understanding and seated himself.

"Why don't you stay the night?" Ava suggested. "You can use one of the spare bedrooms." Then as an afterthought, she added, "When you are warmed through, you can go bring your truck around and park it in one of the garages."

Gerry was about to argue, until Ava gave him a glare.

"Well, if it's alright between you both," Alex replied hesitantly seeing the sullen look on Gerry's face as he thumped the tumbler of whiskey down onto the table. "It would mean I could get an earlier start in the morning."

"Well, now that's settled, after you have brought your car around and parked it in the garage, Gerry will show you to your room."

Alex finished his drink then got up and followed Gerry out into the hall where he donned his already wet clothing and went outside into the driving snow.

Before Alex left, Gerry pointed out that there was access straight from the garage into the house. And he would also open the electronic gates to let him through. As soon as he was outside the garages, he must sound the horn, then he would open the garage doors to let him in. Gerry added that didn't want the garages filled with snow.

Alex thanked him and made his way through the deep snow towards his vehicle, then stopped when seeing a woman and young girl walking by just a few yards away from him.

"Hello!" he called. "Can I give you a lift anywhere?" he shouted hoping that she had heard him through the noise of the blustery wind. The woman stopped and turned, gave a sad smile then to Alex's surprise, she and the child disappeared into the falling snow.

"Oh boy," he whispered tugging at the car door and reaching in to grab his camera then stopped when realising that it was too late to get a photo.

"Damn," he muttered at the missed opportunity. He climbed into his vehicle, then turned it around and drove through the gates and into the garage, where Gerry was stood waiting impatiently for him.

As soon as Alex got out of his truck, Gerry beckoned for him to follow him into the house. Then he begrudgingly told Alex to remove his wet clothing and advised him that after he had shown him to his room, he must shower and change before lunch.

By now, Alex was seething at Gerry's demeaning attitude towards him and was forcing himself to keep his anger under control. He picked up his backpack and slung it over his shoulder, then keeping a few steps behind Gerry, he went up the winding staircase. Then stopped as soon as they were halfway across the balcony.

"Gerry, wait."

Gerry stopped and held his breath, wondering what Alex was about to say.

"There's a woman standing between us here on the balcony."

"What? Where is she? Oh god," Gerry gasped then dropped into silence when he turned around and found himself face to face with the unidentified woman in blue. For a few seconds, he was speechless then turned and ran screaming down the stairs. To Alex's surprise, the woman then turned and gazed towards him. Although he couldn't see her face, he could feel her eyes boring directly into his.

In no time at all, Alex was rendered motionless; he couldn't move and watched as she slowly floated across the balcony to the foot of the attic staircase and disappeared.

Ava, who had heard the commotion, hurried from the lounge and was just in time to see Gerry, white-faced and in a blind panic, race past her into his office then heard the door slam and the key turn in the lock.

"Gerry, speak to me! What's happened?" she yelled pulling at the door handle. "Gerry…"

"We've both seen her," Alex spoke calmly, coming down the stairs to Ava's side. "Your husband panicked and ran when he saw her standing in front of him."

Ave let go of the door handle.

"He's seen her before," she said. "But she is usually watching us from the balcony."

"Has she ever put in an appearance anywhere else?" Alex asked.

"We are not certain it is her, but at times as you are aware, there is no daylight filtering through into the dark areas of the passages, so we are unsure what we are seeing is her. Sometimes the shapes that appear in the gloomy shadows look like people who are moving about the house."

"I understand," Alex began pacing thoughtfully about the lobby then, stopped and held up his finger. "Did they disappear when you switched on the light?" he asked.

"Yes, that is why we thought we were imagining things. We have also heard the sound of men's footsteps walking past our bedroom door at night. And we have actually caught sight of a woman who is sobbing as she moves across the balcony towards the staircase leading up to the attic, she disappears though when reaching the foot of the staircase."

Alex paused for a moment before asking if the house had been blessed before they moved in.

Ava informed him that she wasn't certain, although the builder had mentioned something about old souls being laid to rest at the Grange. But she hadn't understood what he was talking about as both herself and Gerry had been too busy organising where to put the furniture when moving into the Grange.

Alex nodded, "I'd better get showered and changed, then we will talk when your husband is feeling better."

Chapter 26
The Briefing

Alex left Ava to sort out her husband while he went upstairs to the room Gerry had pointed out to him and went inside to get cleaned up and change.

"So this is how the other half live," he murmured to himself when seeing the huge centrally placed double bed that was covered with a silk hand-embroidered eiderdown. On one side of the bedroom was a matching three-seater sofa with two reclining chairs and two low coffee tables.

Four Chippendale chairs were set about the bedroom and two highly polished sideboards were placed on either side of the door. Another door led into the walk-in wardrobe while the other door opened into a spacious bathroom. This consisted of two sinks set in a marble top with cupid handled cupboards running along one wall. In the centre of the room was a cast iron bath set on lion clawed feet along with brass taps and plug. In the opposite corner was a double shower complete with brass fittings, and a toilet with a full floral design both inside and out.

Adding to the luxurious accommodation were a number of thick deep pile carpets scattered about the tiled bathroom floor. A heated towel rail complete with bath and hand towels plus a white bath robe hung from decorative hooks set in a mahogany rail fitted to the tiled wall.

After adjusting the surprise of where he would be sleeping, and not outside in his tent, Alex hesitantly picked up his damp backpack and opened it up on the bathroom floor where he wouldn't spoil the fitted bedroom carpet.

He took out a pair of clean jeans, t-shirt and sweater and hung them on the clothes hooks before taking a hot relaxing shower. After drying himself, Alex set about dressing, he shaved with the small razor he always carried with him and combed his hair. Then after assuring himself that he was presentable, he picked up his camcorder and went downstairs to join Ava and Gerry.

After lunch was over, the three of them settled down to work out a plan of action. They decided that as it became dark by four o clock, almost every light in the house should be turned on to enable them to work in safety. It would also help them see where they were going and discern whatever could be a danger to them.

Alex was already charging up the batteries for the two camcorders in his room, along with other electrical pieces of equipment they would be needing.

He had pointed out earlier to Gerry and Ava that before they started the investigation, he would be performing a protective ritual around them.

"Most people," he explained, "don't realise that they need protection as there are bad spirit as well as good waiting to be released. For a spirit to appear, it needs to use the electrical impulses generated from the recipient's body in order to make itself seen. In our studies, we have also discovered that electricity can be generated from any electrical appliances especially the main electrical circuit. It is the same with UFO activity, they all need electricity to put in an appearance."

Alex pointed to a small unit that he pulled from his pocket. "This little gadget will tell us if there is something sending out electrical waves, and by the way all house phones, mobile phones, TV's, radio, anything sending out electrical impulses must be switched off as the signals could interfere with the equipment we will be using. Now, are there any questions you wish to ask?"

"Do we have to turn off the fridge and freezers?"

"No," Alex replied, turning to Ava.

"What do we do if more than one ghost appears?" she asked hesitantly. "What if it is someone who was close? A relative or such."

Alex was just about to answer when Gerry interrupted, "She means our boys, or my sister," he announced grimly.

"Then we will deal with that if we come to it. Some of the spirit people don't realise they are dead and stick to a regular routine, while others who are stuck between both periods of time need help to pass to the other side."

"Is that what's happening here?" Ava questioned.

"I can't answer that for certain," Alex replied, "but it looks like it. When someone has met a death that was totally unexpected, like an accident or murder, or someone who didn't want to die but did, then they will stay and haunt the vicinity where they died. For example, look at the airline pilot whose plane crashed in the Florida swamp some years ago. Parts of the wreckage from his plane that were reusable were put into other aircraft, but the attendants in those aircraft swore blind that the planes were haunted after seeing the dead pilot moving about the aircraft and they refused to fly in them."

"Then there's the apparitions being seen at the side of the road where accidents have occurred, some unsuspecting motorists have actually given them a lift, the drivers have been scared out of their wits when their passenger has suddenly disappeared."

"There are people who have committed suicide, many of them haven't really wanted to die and it has been a cry for help. Soldiers who have died in wars still haunt the battlefields, brides or brides to be of these men who couldn't live without them haunt the places where they died. In years past when family feuds were a common occurrence, the wealthy parents wanted their offspring to marry into money, but due to the parents feuding the children involved were banned from meeting one another and killed themselves. I could go on forever with causes for hauntings."

"What about those things who mess with people's minds and move or throw things about?" Gerry asked.

"You mean poltergeist."

Gerry nodded.

"I wouldn't worry too much about those, I don't sense any here. My concern is for the lady in blue who walks along the balcony and stops at the foot of the attic staircase. She is the one who is desperately trying to tell you something."

"What about the young man who I saw in my study?" Ava asked. "He was definitely looking for someone whom he could recognise."

"Have you seen him since?" Alex enquired. Unbeknown to Ava, Alex had been delving into the property's history before he came to the Grange, and had a vague idea about of whom the man could be.

"Yes, I have," she replied, "but only from a distance; he is watching me though," Ava paused for a moment. "I know that this is going to sound silly but it's as if he somehow recognises me."

Before she could say anymore, Alex butted in, "Will it be alright for me to do some filming?" he asked, totally ignoring Ava.

"I have a more sensitive camcorder than yours that I use for work. Ava can use the smaller one that we have for recording family movies, and I also have a handgun."

"What?" Alex responded sharply.

"You don't have to worry, it is licenced."

Alex could feel his temper rising and fought hard to control the emotions raging through him, thinking, *the silly bugger doesn't realise that a gun would be useless against a ghost.*

Gerry had insisted that once the investigation was begun, he would be leading the way with both Alex and Ava filming behind, while he himself videoed up front.

"They would," he said, "be filming where every detailed sighting had occurred in the manor."

In the meantime, while they had been making their plans and discussing their strategy, Jenny the cleaner who hadn't wanted to disturb them before she left, had kindly prepared the evening meal and had already started a joint roasting in the oven. All Ava had to do was turn on the hobs and cook the vegetables.

By the time they had finished their discussion, Ava had already started the veg cooking, and when everything was ready and set on the table, Gerry opened a quality bottle of claret to accompany the roast venison. Then by seven o clock that evening, they had finished the meal and were comfortably seated in the lounge drinking coffee.

Chapter 27
Proof

While relaxing in the lounge after the sumptuous meal, Alex asked if he could supply them with some proof of his spiritual abilities, whereby Ava readily agreed to hearing what he had to say.

To Ava's surprise, Alex asked about her cousin Simon, who had died in a motorcycle accident when she was six years old. Ava could hardly believe what she was hearing; how could he possibly know about what had happened all those years ago? But most surprising of all was Alex knowing Simon's name.

Before she had the opportunity to reply, Alex turned his attention to Gerry and asked about his friend Bernard, with whom he had attended university and had shared a dorm.

As soon as Bernard's name was mentioned, Ava noticed Gerry blanch and go pale, and for a few moments, he sat staring blankly at Alex.

Alex waited a while before letting Gerry know that Bernard was sorry for what he had done. He said that in a state of depression after discovering he had flunked all of his grades, Bernard had taken his own life.

Gerry was dumbfounded; he had never spoken of the tragedy not even to Ava. It was something that Gerry had put out of his mind and Bernard was now just a faded memory.

"My God, how did you know about Bernard?" Gerry stammered. "I mean—"

"It's alright, they are here with you, there's nothing to fear from them, they are here to help you."

Gerry's jaw tensed. "How the bloody hell can they be of help when they're dead?"

"Gerry please," Ava moved forward taking hold of his arm. "Alex is only trying to help, for goodness sake," she argued, trying not to lose her temper with her husband's outlandish behaviour. "He is giving us proof, isn't he, what more do you want?"

"I want to forget the fucking past, that's what I want," he seethed when recalling the sickening sight of Bernard's body dangling from the light fitting in front of him when he opened the door to the dorm.

"Gerry, please, for once in your life, will you please consider other people and control yourself?" Ava snapped in an effort to calm the situation.

Gerry pushed her hand away from his arm and turned to seat himself in the chair where he sat staring into the blazing fire. His immediate thoughts had gone to the apparition of the shabbily clothed stable boy grooming the horse in the barn.

As if reading his thoughts, Alex asked about the courtyard and stables that used to stand just a short distance away from the Hall.

"I don't know about them," Gerry replied in a sullen tone. "Jack Armstrong the builder must have cleared the whole area before we arrived, but there is a row of stone buildings just a short distance away from the Grange. Those were here when we purchased the property. You can see them from the house right now but he told us that they are hidden from sight in the summertime when the trees and bushes are covered with foliage."

Alex nodded. "Perhaps we could go take a look at them later. My main concern is here in the Grange itself, mainly the attic and the cellar from where I believe the hauntings are emanating."

Chapter 28
The Investigation

By seven am the following morning, after Ava, Gerry and Alex had finished breakfast, Gerry led Alex out of the lounge and into the wide open area towards the staircase with Ava following close behind. They moved quietly up the stairs, along the balcony and past the bedrooms until reaching the oppressive, dark twisting staircase leading to the attic.

"We are going to need some light up here," Gerry said, switching on the lights. "This part of the house is pretty dark and if you haven't already noticed there are no windows for the daylight to come through and we only have three low-voltage wall lights up here."

Alex nodded. "I see what you mean. What the devil?" he suddenly exclaimed, when the lights began flickering then faded away into nothing and an eerie silence ensued.

"Oh shit," Gerry moaned.

"Something's happening here," Alex warned putting a restraining hand on Gerry's arm to stop him from moving any further. "Switch on the camcorder and start filming."

"There's nothing to see," Gerry whispered, glancing fearfully about the oppressive area.

"Let me be the judge of that. Now focus the camera straight ahead and the camera will show if anything is there."

"But there's nothing there," Gerry whinged pathetically.

"Shut up and do as I say, the camera can see things we can't," Alex snapped, annoyed by Gerry's simpering attitude.

Alex reached into his pocket and took out the small infra-red torch and the gadget he had brought along in the hope of unlocking the attic door. Gerry, who was two steps up ahead of Alex, suddenly stopped and couldn't move. Ava gave a muffled cry and pointed towards the top of the dark staircase.

"Oh my God," he gasped when seeing a veiled woman dressed in a silver blue gown standing in a shimmering halo of bright light, poised with her hand resting on the door handle facing Gerry.

Dazzled by the blinding haze she was creating, Alex turned his gaze away then felt his jaw drop at the sight of a ragged urchin dragging himself across the landing before disappearing through the bedroom wall.

"What the hell's happening here!" Alex yelled in confusion as he spun around, not knowing which way to turn, when a number of weird unearthly shapes began forming around them. There were so many shapes and shadows encircling them that Alex found it hard to focus on one specific being.

"I don't bloody know," Gerry yelled. "But as far as I'm concerned, I'm getting out of here and if you've got any sense, you'll come with me."

"But what about the attic?" Alex shouted in a loud voice that echoed into the eerie silence.

"You go up if you want to," Gerry called as he pushed Ava in front of him from halfway across the balcony. "You can't get in there, even the builder couldn't get in there, see for yourself; it's double locked and there isn't a key to fit it."

Amidst the confusion, the ghostly apparition of the woman disappeared, leaving a clear passage for Alex, to bound up the rest of the staircase, while Gerry and Ava raced down the stairs as fast as their legs would carry them.

Alex's concentration was so deeply focused in trying to open the antiquated locks that he was oblivious to what was happening behind him until, sensing danger, he heard harsh, snarling, sounds coming from behind him and turned.

"Oh shit," he yelled when seeing two massive Irish wolfhounds on the staircase behind him, blocking his only means of escape.

"Gerry! Gerry! Help me!" he called frantically not daring to take his eyes away from the ferocious snarling beasts' drooling fangs.

"Oh God, this is worse than I expected," he groaned, when seeing the vicious animals' ears flatten behind their heads and the hair rising along their spine as if about to attack.

"Come on, man, think," he muttered to himself. "They're not real! They are ghosts; they won't harm you."

Although he was terrified by what he was seeing, Alex suddenly became aware of his spirit guide taking control and sending a sense of strength filtering through him.

"Away with you!" he shouted at the top of his voice. "You are not real, you belong with the dead."

The instant he uttered these words, the creatures disappeared allowing Alex to race down the staircase and within seconds he was standing by Gerry's side in the hallway.

Gerry could feel the tremors of fear rushing through Alex's body as he ushered him towards the lounge.

"I think we all need a drink after that," he suggested when seeing the ghastly pallor of Alex's face. "Do you want coffee, or would you prefer something stronger?" he asked.

"Whiskey, if you don't mind," Alex managed to utter in a stunned tone. "I don't usually drink while I'm working, but by God, I need it now."

For the first time in carrying out a psychic investigation, Alex felt himself unable to restrain the supernatural power that had built up over the years at the Grange. He knew from his past experiences of dealing with phenomena that this was something big. It was also something that was completely beyond his understanding and out of his control.

Alex realised and understood that he would be needing help from his investigative team, as it was something he couldn't do alone. The hauntings were too strong and powerful for one person to overcome single-handed.

While he was stood perplexed and deep in thought, Gerry hurried into the kitchen to set up the coffee. Ava, noticing the pensive look on Alex's face, had taken hold of his arm and led him over to the fireside and seated him in one of the comfortable armchairs.

"Can I get you another drink?" Ava offered indicating towards the bar.

"I'm alright thanks, Gerry's sorting it out," he replied.

Just then Gerry entered the lounge with the coffee and placed the tray onto the table in front of Alex, then went over to the bar and poured himself a tumbler full of whiskey and a cognac for Ava.

"Isn't it a little early in the day for you to be drinking, Gerry?"

"No darling," he replied in a patronising tone as he handed her the cognac. "It isn't, not after what I've seen upstairs."

"I think you are forgetting that I was up there with you but not for long—you turned tail and ran."

Gerry threw her a scathing look and seated himself by the window. "It didn't take long for you to follow, did it?" he snapped.

Alex listened to them bickering for a while before asking if either of them had seen the two Irish wolfhounds on the landing?

"No," Ava replied, "but two of our friends saw them a few nights ago when we held the house-warming party."

Alex didn't say anymore for a while, then asked Gerry. "Why have you avoided taking me into the cellar?"

"Have I," Gerry feigned puzzlement at the sudden unexpected question.

"Yes, you have," Alex replied nodding his head.

"I didn't realise, sorry," Gerry muttered trying to avoid answering. "To be honest, I'd completely forgotten about the cellar."

Chapter 29
The Cellar

"Do you want to go back upstairs?" Gerry asked hesitantly when they had all calmed down.

"No," Alex replied a little too quickly. "I think I we should wait until I call the rest of my team to help out here, to be honest I think the Grange is too dangerous for just one person to investigate on his own."

"If you say so."

Gerry got up from the chair and walked towards the door. "How long will it take for your friends to arrive and how many will there be?" he asked.

"There are three, two women and one man. All are psychic and understand the workings of the electrical equipment they will be bringing. I will also be asking your permission for us to set up cameras about the Grange, and you don't have to worry about accommodating extra people. We carry our own tents, sleeping bags and food supplies. It will take about a week for them to pack everything we need and to get here."

"That's fine by me," Ava replied, "what do you say, Gerry?"

"It doesn't matter whether I agree or not; you will do as you like," Gerry replied with a shrug. "Make the arrangements," he told Alex. "Just make sure they bring clean shoes."

Ava groaned.

"Come on," he said indicating for Alex to follow, "we're going to the cellar."

Alex got up from the chair and followed Gerry down the long corridor until they reached the cellar door. But as soon as Gerry opened the door and reached inside to switch on the light, he felt something cold and bony touch his hand. Startled, he quickly pulled his arm back and glanced at Alex who was watching every move he made.

"Did you see or feel anything?" he asked tremulously.

"Yes, I did, it was extremely cold and fast, there is no doubt whatsoever it was, was certainly wanting to make its presence known."

"Oh shit," Gerry groaned, "I think we should get back to Ava."

"No! We have to face whatever or whoever is down there; otherwise they will never find peace. It will stay in purgatory for the rest of time and the evil forces will grow stronger and control the people's minds living here."

For a few moments, the men stood looking at one another before Gerry decided to face whatever was in the cellar.

"You win," he said hesitantly before reopening the cellar door, Gerry then grasped his camcorder firmly and began filming straight ahead, but was too afraid to reach inside to switch on the light.

"Do you want to go first?"

Alex declined, shaking his head, leaving Gerry no option but to move forward into the pitch blackness onto the cellar steps. Alex, however, was only testing Gerry and had switched on the infrared torch that he always carried and shone the beam into the cellar directly ahead of him. Thankfully, the area was clear allowing Gerry to reach over to the switch and turn on the light.

He gave an audible sigh of relief when the light flooded the first area of the massive cellar and seeing no one was standing there waiting for them.

"Come on, be careful, the handrail is a bit loose." Gerry carefully led the way down the stone steps until reaching the bottom and they were standing in the first area of the cellar.

"There's another light for back there," Gerry pointed towards another space in the cellar. "But we don't often use that area."

Alex was amazed by the size of the cellar, the low stone arches supporting the building above created dark shadows in the alcoves that spread at different angles across the massive cellar. To the sides of the walls were a number of cells with padlocked iron gates.

"How far back does the cellar go?" Alex asked staring into the darker area beyond them. "And why are there padlocked cells down here?"

Before Gerry had the chance to reply, Alex grabbed hold of Gerry's arm and indicated towards the darker area ahead of them. "Wait! Look!" he whispered. "Something's moving over there."

Gerry peered into the darkness. "I can't see anything," he replied in a hushed voice.

"Have you got the video working?" Alex asked in a low tone. "I could swear I saw a something moving over there." Alex indicated towards the distant far wall.

"Yes," Gerry replied softly. "What was it?"

"I don't rightly know, but whatever it was had a strange dull glow and it disappeared through that Wall. Come on, let's take a look over there."

"We never come into this part; well I don't; and Ava flatly refuses to come into the cellar."

Gerry moved reluctantly forward into the empty area.

"Don't you store anything here?" Alex asked gazing about the vast empty space. "There's plenty of room back here. If the Grange was ever turned into flats, you could earn a fortune. Oh boy, look at that." Alex could hardly conceal his excitement, and hurried over to the stone wall where he had noticed a slight discrepancy in the stonework and began running his fingers over it. Then leapt back when he felt a cold hand touching his from behind the stone block wall. For a few moments, he was shocked and stared at the wall then slowly retreated.

"Gerry, come here, take a look at this wall, I think I've found something. Look at the cement between the stones, it's lighter here than the rest of the wall. And I felt something touch me when I examined the stone."

Gerry moved to where Alex was standing, and under close examination he could just make out a difference in the colour of the cement between the blocks of stone that Alex was referring to, and began tracing the whole area with his hands.

"It looks as if three quarters of the wall has been rebuilt," he said scanning the wall thoughtfully. "I wish I could afford to knock it down and take a look behind, but I can't. Anyway, we don't know if the area is safe behind, do we?"

"You may be right; it could be dangerous." Alex paused as he contemplated what they could do.

"I'll tell you what, maybe we could contact the people who rebuilt this wall and ask them what was behind it. Was it full of rubble? Or was there a way through to the rear of the building. You did say that Jack Armstrong had arranged the cellar's structure so that it could be more convenient for you to use."

"Well, we can't ask Jack."

"Why not?"

"Because he's dead. I found his body; he was frozen to death in his car and from the look of sheer terror on his face, I don't want to know what killed him either. Not only that, he was dead when he let us into the house."

Alex stared at him in amazement. "You mean a ghost let you inside the mansion?"

"Too bloody true," Gerry spluttered.

"My God," Alex whispered in a strained voice before asking, "Did you ever look into the history of the Grange before you purchased it, and about its past owners."

"No," Gerry shook his head, confused by the questions. "I got it for a bargain price, believe it or not. It came at a lesser price than the new houses at the bottom of Gallows Hill, and it is three or maybe four times the size of those."

"I can believe that with its past history, but as you will understand, there will have been many tragedies and deaths here over the years," Alex replied.

Gerry nodded in agreement.

"I have also checked out the full history of the Manor." Alex remarked knowingly, and informed Gerry of the research that he had carried out, back to the time when the first Lord Goldberg had purchased the land.

"However, the one event that intrigues me the most is, what happened to the young Lord Goldberg who disappeared after he raped his own daughter. It was recorded that he rode out onto the moors and was never seen again. The search parties never found his body, although I don't believe they gave a damn about what had happened to him after what he did."

Gerry gave a sanctimonious huff. "Would you want to find an abomination like him?"

"No, not really," Alex replied, "but could I ask you a question before we go back upstairs?"

"Yes, what is it?"

"Is your wife Ava a sensitive?"

"A sensitive what?" Gerry frowned, puzzled by the question.

"Never mind just now."

Gerry hadn't given it a second thought when he and Ava had first moved into the property, but when they had gone into the cellar, Ava said that she must have been imagining things when she believed that she saw a man disappear through the cellar wall.

They both agreed that she must have been exhausted after the move and in getting everything prepared for the children's homecoming. Ava however, did not say anything to Gerry about feeling someone place a cold feminine hand on her arm as well.

Ava had had enough, and she didn't stay while Gerry investigated the rest of the cellar, she returned to the comforting sounds of the removal men chatting to one another as they placed the furniture in its allocated places.

Back in the cellar Gerry had found it rather odd when he noticed there were small cells on either side of the cellar walls, that each had a steel barred gate and still contained a lock. And the key for each lock was hung on the wall outside of each cell.

Also, with the cellar being wide and long there were separate light switches for different areas of the low arched construction. Therefore, when looking into the darkened areas the light from other vicinities cast weird shapes and shadows amongst the items stored there.

Gerry had been surprised when, as he had passed from one cell to the other, he'd discovered that each cell was jam packed with relics from the past. Old fashioned mangles and other obsolete washing equipment was stored there, along with worn out and unused sweeping brushes; dust pans; gardening tools; a number of old sit up and beg bicycles; prams; children's toys; large, sealed wooden crates, and unopened boxes covered with cobwebs and dust, plus candles and rusty old oil lamps.

Gerry found himself wondering why the builder hadn't removed them.

But before he had the opportunity to investigate further, he heard Ava calling to him and returned upstairs to assist her with setting up the furniture and instructing the removal men where they required the items placing. He had made a point to remind himself that when he had the time, he would have the handrail replaced as it was loose in its settings, making it dangerous.

Chapter 30
History of the Hall

"Gerry, are you alright?" a voice broke into his thoughts, when he saw Alex staring at him with a worried look on his face.

"What? Er yes," he stammered. "What where you saying?"

"I was asking if Ava was a sensitive?" he replied. "I definitely know that she has seen something that has upset her badly, hasn't she?"

Alex waited for Gerry to offer an explanation, and after a few minutes of thought, he told Alex about the weird encounter that Ava had experienced a few days ago.

"I thought as much," he said nodding his head. "Well, I can definitely tell you there is a strong presence down here whose soul isn't at peace. To be honest, they think that they're still alive and are seeking revenge. Have you seen or noticed anything unusual when you're down here at any time?"

"No, I haven't, but wait a minute, Jack Armstrong the builder did mention that some of his men had refused to work in the cellar. They were too scared to work down there after seeing more than one figure go floating through the wall."

"I have studied the history of Goldberg Hall and it isn't nice," Alex told him. "In the 1800s, when the fire broke out that destroyed most of Goldberg Hall, the owner of the Mansion at the time was Viscount Basil Blackmore. It is rumoured that he was in a foul mood and drunk when the fire broke out that destroyed the biggest part of the building."

"He'd had to sell most of the family's valuable antiques and was forced to close the biggest part of the Hall as he had no money to pay the servants for its upkeep. He had also gambled the hall away when he lost it to a Lord Jeffries in a game of poker."

"Before he was forced to leave the Hall, luckily for everyone involved at the time of the fire, there were only two servants left in the household who managed to escape the blaze. They told the investigators that he had deliberately caused the fire when he set light to the drapes after he had thrown the paraffin table lamps to the floor. The spilt paraffin had sent flames racing across the carpets and wooden floors. The last they saw of him he was screaming and racing around the hall with a lighted candelabra in his hands setting fire to everything he could."

"He had, in their opinion, gone completely mad. It was understood that he was the only person to perish in the flames."

"Most of the mansion had collapsed into the cellar during the fire which gutted the biggest part of the building. This part of the mansion is all that's left, thankfully, it was only partially damaged during the fire."

"I would like to bet though that someone else was in here when the fire started," Alex added with a grimace. "Then when the old Hall collapsed, they could have been trapped beneath the rubble when it dropped into the cellar. I wonder if they ever did find Lord Blackmore's body? Did you know that Lord Jeffries disappeared around about the same time?"

"No, I didn't, I have no idea what happened to Jeffries, nor Blackmore," Gerry replied. "I presumed that he must have been buried beneath the rubble when the building collapsed."

"That means they never discovered if he was dead or not after the fire," Alex added thoughtfully. "He could have escaped and run away; you must never underestimate his sort, the landed gentry and politicians look after their own. They also have vast fortunes stashed away that we don't know of, and when the worst comes to the worst, they hide one another in different countries."

"It's the same today look at a certain Lord who murdered the wrong woman. He thought he was killing his wife but where did he go? Somebody must have got him out of the country. It's hard to believe that Jeffries died and Lord Goldberg disappeared on the Moors." Alex hesitated dramatically for a moment.

"If Blackmore didn't die in the fire, did he kill the person who was about to take possession of the Hall, then set fire to the Hall to cover up the murder he had committed? When the charred corpse had been found after the fire, it would have been presumed to be Blackmore's, but if it wasn't his, then who's was it, and who is haunting the cellar?"

"Good question," Gerry couldn't help but admire Alex for expressing himself so clearly. "Your guess is as good as mine," he added thoughtfully.

To his surprise, Alex abruptly changed the subject.

"It must have been a very imposing building in its day. On the old deeds in the archives," Alex continued, "they show that there were over eighty rooms in the mansion, with a large pebbled courtyard, stables for horses, hunting dogs, coach house and whatever was necessary for the upkeep of the property. Plus, a large, number of servants."

"Did you know," he said, "that during the first and second world wars, they used to house the troops here and they were billeted in the small cells set on either side of the cellar?"

Alex waited for a few moments for Gerry to respond to what he was saying, but when Gerry didn't say anything, Alex carried on, "They also used the cellars in the 1940s for people who were being evacuated from the asylums in the cities that were in danger of being bombed by the enemy. The government didn't want the lunatics running around causing mayhem if they escaped the bombing, the public had enough to worry about. That was why locks were placed on each cell and throughout the entire household."

"Bloody hell, I didn't know that," Gerry uttered in amazement. "This place has certainly held some mysteries its past."

"There have also been numerous suicides at Goldberg Hall throughout history," Alex informed him. "Some of the owners killed themselves when they lost the property due to gambling debts and over-spending. Also those parasites were seldom sober and most of the time were drugged out of their nasty minds, with opium and other paraphernalia. They were living off their parents' ill-gotten gains," Alex finished with a grimace before adding further, "There is worse to come."

"What do you mean?" Gerry asked, his mind agog with what Alex was telling him.

Alex took a deep breath before continuing, "It is written that when the lords got together and felt they needed a different type of pleasure, young children, both boys and girls, were brought in to gratify their perverted needs. Young serving maids were forced into illicit sex and some became pregnant during the orgies, or fell ill with a sexually transmitted disease from their assailants and they took their own lives."

"The children who escaped told the authorities that they were forcibly taken to the Hall and forced to do unnatural things with animals and with the lords, who were often drunken beasts themselves."

"The landed gentry didn't give a damn about the poor working class people, they just took their children whenever they wanted. The poor sods who lived in the tied cottages owned by the lords were too afraid to speak out for fear of losing their lives. And the magistrates didn't pursue the children's stories of abuse, as they were amongst the abusers."

"How do you know all of this?" Gerry asked, in awe of what Alex was saying.

"I'll come to that in a minute. When the Lords of the manors sent out their hired henchmen to collect the youngsters for the orgies, the children's parents would often hide them away, but those who couldn't be hidden were taken. Some were never seen again, there was also talk of black satanic rituals where babies were sacrificed to the god Baphomet."

Gerry was knocked speechless by what he was hearing.

"Wasn't Baphomet something to do with the Templars movement?" he asked in bewilderment.

"Right first time," Alex agreed. "In some of their rituals, they drank the blood of their victims and resorted to cannibalism."

"Oh my God." Gerry could hardly believe what he was hearing. "Where did you hear about this? I mean who...?" he garbled unable to ask a straight question.

"Bill Jackson the village smithy, he's lived here all his life and the stories have been handed down through each generation. But there is also damning written evidence that is kept at the local library about what the gentry got up to and participated in."

Chapter 31
Mary and Susan

Ava gave a sigh of relief when her friend Sarah rang asking if she would care to meet up with three of their neighbours at the local tea rooms-cum-post office, grocery store and newsagent. To be honest, Ava was grateful for the opportunity to get away from the house and let Gerry and Alex carry on with their investigations in the cellar.

As she slowly made her way down the deep snow-covered lane carefully treading in the ruts made by Jake's tractor, Ava noticed a young woman wearing a medium length brown padded jacket with a hood, ankle boots, jeans and a furry hat. She was talking to a little girl dressed in a pink jacket, pink bonnet and pale brown leggings who was aged about seven years old.

"Hello," Ava called, reaching her side. "I'm Ava Banks. I live at the grange back there," she half turned and pointed towards the house.

The woman stopped walking and turned to face her. "I'm Mary Nelson," she said introducing herself, "and this is my daughter Susan."

"Hello Susan, I'm Ava, I hope we're going to become friends," Ava said, leaning down and taking the little girl's hand, then quickly withdrew her own hand when noticing how cold and stiff the child's fingers were.

"My goodness, you're cold, why don't the two of you come and have a nice cup of tea with me and my friends?" she offered, noticing the pale faces of both mother and child.

"We can't," Susan said. "Mummy is taking me to see the three waterfalls down Waterfall Lane, aren't you, Mummy?"

"Yes dear, I am," Mary spoke softly to the child. "I always keep my promise, don't I?"

"Yes, Mummy." The child gave a hop and a skip in front of them both. She had never been allowed near the river and was filled with excitement at the thought of seeing the water for the first time.

Ava watched as they turned into Waterfall Lane and smiled at the child's enthusiasm for visiting the river, and made her way to the tearooms where everyone was sat waiting for her arrival.

"Sorry I got held up," she said removing her coat and hung it over the hanger provided then seated herself. The waitress came over to take their order as she began explaining about Mary and Susan.

Maria's jaw dropped and Anna almost gagged when she asked. "You were talking to them?"

"Well, yes. Why? Why shouldn't I? They were on their way—"

"Oh my God, don't say anymore, haven't you heard any of the local gossip?" Donna asked in a serious tone.

"What is it? What's wrong?" Ava stuttered, looking around at the stunned faces staring at her.

It was the waitress, Alice Thomson, who broke the numbing silence. "Mary Nelson drowned herself and Susan in Waterfall River five years ago, the doctor said that she was suffering from depression. But in most people's opinion, she was never right after seeing something up at the old Hall. That was shortly before Jack Armstrong began building the new houses and renovating the old place."

"Even Jack and his men didn't like working on it, they all saw something up there but wouldn't say what it was. Have you ever wondered how the road Gallows Hill got its name?" she asked turning the conversation.

"No," Ava replied shaking her head in confusion. "I just presumed that was its name, I never thought anymore about it."

"In the olden days," Alice said, then beamed as Ava, Anne, Lucy and Donna turned towards her as did a number of the customers in the café, "they used to hang people at the top of the hill where you live," she said with a sombre expression on her face.

"Old Ezra Goldberg who built the Hall, that is now 'The Grange', was the presiding judge over every trial in this area, and he was known as the Hanging Judge. Whether they poor sods were guilty of a crime or not, he always found an excuse to condemn most of the prisoners to death. If it wasn't for theft then it was witchcraft, and some were sent abroad to only the devil knows where."

"He was an evil old bugger, just like his sons and grandsons. The prison was built where some of you live! You know where the twelve new houses are. And the cellars at the old hall were used for torturing others who wouldn't give up certain secrets. He said the peasants were conspiring to get rid of him and his family and that's why he killed them."

Ava was speechless, as were the other women by Alice's revelations.

"I'll tell you something else," she said. "Jack Armstrong has been seen wandering around the village ever since he died, and he's been seen in here. In fact, he's been seen sitting at the window table where you're seated now, and on Gallows Hill."

Alice turned away smiling smugly to herself when seeing the stunned looks on the faces of Ava and her friends, with the knowledge that she now had them all worrying about the gruesome atrocities carried out in the area where they were now living.

"Bloody outsiders, that should put them off staying, we don't want them here," Alice muttered beneath her breath as she walked away to place their orders.

Chapter 32
The Woman in Black

Ava was working like crazy designing book covers for the latest magazine, and for Sally's homecoming from boarding school that was due in three days. She had told Gerry about the conversation in the tearooms, but he had told her to forget about it as she had better things to do than waste time worrying about what had happened in the past.

What Ava had told him about Gallows Hill however, caused him to think about the stable lad he and Michael had seen in the barn grooming the horse. Also the weird apparition who had left no footprints in the snow. Was all of that a reminder of the past, Gerry wondered.

He gave an involuntary shudder at the memory then shook his head and carried on working.

By lunchtime, Ava had completed her graphic design and was preparing sandwiches in the kitchen and called to Gerry telling him that it was almost ready. But when he didn't answer, she went out in the hall summon him, then stopped and listened when hearing a rustling sound coming from above.

"Oh no," she murmured, glancing up towards the first floor balcony, and was startled to see a veiled woman dressed entirely in black staring down at her from above.

"Oh my God," Ava whispered turning her gaze away from the woman, then rushed into Gerry's office where she found him fast asleep.

"Gerry, Gerry," Ava hissed, shaking his shoulder. "There's someone upstairs, it's a woman."

"What?" he mumbled sleepily. "Where is she?"

"She's upstairs on the balcony, I think she's a ghost."

"Don't talk daft, ring the police while I go and find out what she's up to." Gerry leapt to his feet and headed out of his office, grabbing the first thing he could use as a defensive weapon before stealthily making his way up the staircase.

Meanwhile, as Ava was on the phone to the police, she glanced out of the window and let out a shriek of fear and dropped the phone, upon seeing a gaunt, hollow-cheeked man dressed in rags, with watery, colourless eyes staring at her through the window.

"Oh my God!" she screamed. At that moment, the dispatcher put her frantic call through to the police who had been patrolling the area. They had heard her screams down the phone and raced to the Grange.

Within no time at all, the police arrived outside of the Manor, and two police officers leapt out and hurried to the door. Ava had rushed to unlock and open the door and practically dragged the men inside, then slammed the door shut and locked it behind them.

She ushered the officers into her office, pointing to the window and telling them about the man she had just seen outside.

"If you are quick, you will catch him," she said, frantically looking out of the window for a sign of the man.

The two officers whispered something to one another then split up, one raced upstairs to help Gerry search for the woman, while the other officer dashed outside of the Manor to search for the man. But after a thorough check both inside and outside of the Manor, there was no sign of any intruders.

"Are you certain you saw someone?" one of the officers asked Ava dubiously. "There are no footprints in the snow outside of this room window, where you say that you saw the intruder, nor or there any anywhere near the house except mine."

Ava didn't know what to say and shrugged helplessly, shaking her head.

"We'd better check those outbuildings," the officer said, giving his colleague a knowing look. "There may be a tramp or somebody hiding in there, you never know."

Ava unlocked the door and watched as the two officers made their way through the deep snow over to the outbuildings and began checking that each door was securely closed. They also took note that the only footprints to be seen were their own, so no one could have been there.

After checking the property thoroughly, they made their way back to the house to report all was clear to Gerry and Ava. When the officers had left the Grange and were sat making notes in the car, Gerry attempted to help Ava feel at ease.

"At least we can be assured that no one is lurking about outside," he said with a smile putting a protective arm around her shoulder. "But I can't imagine who you saw on the upstairs balcony. How was she dressed and what was she wearing?" he asked.

"I will tell you what I saw," she snapped, infuriated by his demeaning attitude. "I saw a middle-aged woman dressed entirely in black, with a veil and a long black cloak staring down at me from the balcony, and there was nothing colourful about her."

"Shit," he muttered to himself when realising that it was the same person he had seen when they had first arrived at the Grange. "I don't want you to worry about it too much," he said, in an attempt to pacify her. "Why don't I make you a nice cup of tea, it will help you relax."

"Tea!" she shrieked, glaring at him and seething with anger. "I saw a bloody ghost, that's what I saw, and not only that, there was another looking at me through the bloody window. And you tell me to have a cup of tea, you must be bloody joking."

Unnoticed by them while they were stood arguing, a second police car had arrived, and a senior police officer stepped from the vehicle and began speaking to the two officers who had checked the property earlier. He then gestured towards the largest of the outbuildings, walked over to it, opened the door and went inside.

Chapter 33
The Disappearing Corpses

Within minutes, Sergeant Dixon reappeared as white as a sheet and threw up the entire contents of his stomach into the snow.

"What's up! What's in there?" Officer Wilks demanded to know from his stricken superior and signalled for Officer Jones to get out of the car to help the distraught Sergeant.

"Don't go in there," Dixon warned, nodding his head towards the open door.

Despite the warning, Jones put his head around the barn door and peered cautiously into the semi darkness of the building before letting out a shriek of alarm. He ran to the police car and rang for emergency backup and an ambulance.

After hearing the raised voices and commotion outside, Gerry told Ava to stay where she was until he had discovered what all the fuss was about. He hurried to the hall cupboard and donned his warm clothing, then hurried outside and leapt through the hedge growth towards the officers.

"I wouldn't advise you to go in, sir," one of them said barring Gerry's way. "It's not a pretty sight."

Gerry hesitated, he recalled what he and Michael had witnessed earlier. But it hadn't caused them to react as the Sergeant had done. Surely he couldn't have witnessed anything other than the stable lad, or could he?

Gerry decided to keep to himself what he had previously seen in there, and stood waiting until the ambulance and extra police had arrived.

"Alright. What's all the fuss about?" Sergeant Brooks demanded to know when he had clambered from the car that had skidded to a halt outside the mansion, along with two ambulances.

"Sir, there's a pile of corpses in there, some are fresh and it appears to me that some look as if they've been there for years," Officer Wilks said tremulously. "Some of the bodies are completely decomposed and rotten."

Brooks threw him a look off total disbelief.

"Let's get in there and see for ourselves, shall we?" Brooks snapped in an authoritative tone, as he marched up to the barn door. Totally ignoring the officers that had now grouped together and were stood waiting and whispering fearfully to one another.

"But sir," Jones faltered as he spoke.

"What?" Sergeant Brooks snapped.

Jones gestured helplessly towards the barn.

"Sir," his voice trembled.

"Come on man, spit it out," he barked.

"There was no one inside the barn a few moments ago when we checked it thoroughly."

"Don't talk so bloody stupid," he snarled turning towards his men. "Come on, pull yourselves together and let's have these doors open," he shouted.

"But Sir," Jones pleaded.

"What is it now?" Brooks snapped turning to face Jones.

"I wouldn't go in there. Sir, if I were you, I'd leave it to the medics."

"Oh you would, would you, well for your information I have seen corpses before," he snapped at the uniformed man.

"But sir, the men don't want to go in there they are scared, it looks as if a full-scale massacre has been carried out in that barn. We've all heard rumours about the unaccountable deaths, murders and suicides, and the ghosts that haunt inside and out of the Manor. Not only that but there's the recent weird unsolved death of Jack Armstrong who within minutes froze to death in his car."

"For God's sake, man, get a grip on yourself, the next thing you will be saying is they've all seen a ghost?"

"I can't say that for certain, Sir, but I can definitely tell you that there are three dead men hanging from the rafters who look as if they have only just been hung. And they weren't there when the barns were first checked; they were all empty."

"What!" Brooks spluttered in amazement.

"Yes sir, and we don't believe they've hung themselves."

"Oh, and how do you reach that conclusion?"

"Because there are no ladders nor anything for them to have stood on to hang themselves with."

For a few moments, the sergeant couldn't believe what he was hearing and stared at the barn, until one of the paramedics who had just arrived asked if it was alright for them to go inside the building, or should they wait for the forensic team to get there.

The sergeant was at a loss at what to say, until another medic pushed his way past them and dashed inside the building. But as speedily as he had entered, he raced out and leant against the doorframe as white as the snow he was standing in.

Not one of the medics had ever witnessed anything akin to the horrific spectacle before them. They stood huddled together outside in the falling snow muttering nervously to one another, looking anywhere but at the barn.

Sergeant Brooks managed to gain control of himself and walked unsteadily back to his car where he put through an urgent call for a forensic team to be sent to the Mansion immediately.

"It's too late for those poor sods now, and by the looks of it, some of those poor buggers on the floor appear to have been skinned while they were still alive," the medic groaned.

After seeing the carnage, he'd collapsed and had to be escorted back to the ambulance where he was being treated for shock by his colleague.

"I think we should get away from here because we can't do anything to help them, and they certainly don't need an ambulance. Let the police sort it out, this is way out of our jurisdiction, they need a specialist team to handle this." He groaned.

His partner agreed and radioed through to base explaining the condition of the decomposed and putrid corpses, and the three dead men suspended from a roof beam with rope around their necks.

At first, the dispatcher couldn't believe what he was hearing, he thought the medics were pulling his leg and laughed. But when he heard the panic in the other man's voice, he realised something was seriously wrong and advised all crews to return to the depot.

Within a short space of time, the whole area was cordoned off and crawling with police. Ava and Gerry were taken into two separate rooms and questioned by two officers. Ava however, couldn't give any answers to what she was being asked.

Gerry finally admitted that he and Michael had seen a stable lad brushing a white stallion that disappeared shortly after he had seen him, also the ghostly figure of the emaciated man who had been watching him in the barn, but didn't leave any footprints in the snow when Gerry had chased after him.

This left the officer shaking his head in disbelief, but he did wonder if it was the same man that Ava had seen looking at her through the window.

Meanwhile, the forensic teams who by now had entered the grimy unlit barn were struggling to make their way around the piles of rancid stinking corpses, old hessian sacks, ropes, carts and other paraphernalia, while huge portable lights were being set in place with some facing the swinging corpses suspended from the roof's sturdy oak beam. When everything was set up and ready for the victims to be photographed before being cut down and the bodies placed on the floor to be examined before removal, to everyone's amazement, the entire area of the floor became void of bodies, and the corpses that had been swinging from the huge oak rafters above suddenly disappeared.

"What the hell's going on here?" the chief medical examiner yelled, jumping to his feet; he could hardly believe his eyes, as one by one the corpses began disappearing.

The police and every member of the forensic team stood watching in awe as every one of the bodies slowly evaporated from sight.

It was hardly surprising that most of the men were now scurrying from the barn before being given permission to leave.

Chapter 34
Possession

Gerry had set up his gymnasium in one of the upper spare rooms, where a strenuous workout was helping him work off the frustration of the past few days. The workouts would also help him to stay fit over the long drawn out winter months before he could get back into training for the All Beef rugby team which he captained. His muscle-bound six foot three physical appearance was enough to deter any player from tackling him.

But at home and when he was working, Gerry appeared to be a different person entirely.

"David, can you give me a hand with those papers on my desk, they are in alphabetical order?" Gerry asked, pointing to a pile of folders. "And put them in my briefcase, I don't want them getting mixed together with those others."

David, who was Gerry's partner, gave Ava a cheeky grin and winked as he went over to the desk to check through the documents before placing them in Gerry's briefcase.

"Sally will be home tomorrow," she said to Gerry who was fumbling about with legal papers.

"I know," he replied in a despondent tone. "And I have to be London for the meeting that couldn't be postponed despite the lousy weather. It looks as if the discussions are going to drag out for quite a few days, in fact it may take a week."

"Oh no," she groaned. "Sally was so looking forward to us all being together this holiday."

"I'm sorry, darling, but there's nothing I can do about it; this is a really special meeting with the backers of the project and I can't miss it. Otherwise some other company will get the job and we need the cash."

"I understand, Gerry," she said quietly holding back a tear, when thinking it would be the first New Year without the boys. "At least I will have some company for the week while you're away."

"Ava, you do understand that if I could avoid going or at least put the meeting back for a few days then I would, just to be with you both, especially after what's been happening around here, with the house and the outbuildings," he responded, splaying his hands in frustration.

"That is something that has been causing me a lot of concern," Ava replied, interrupting what Gerry was about to add.

Her face took on a sombre expression. "I have made a decision that you may not approve of."

"Oh yes?" he said in surprise, glancing towards David who had stopped what he was doing and was listening intently.

Ava took a deep breath as the men looked at her, waiting expectantly for what she was about to say.

"I think we should sell the house, so far it has brought us nothing but bad luck," she began. "To be honest, I am scared most of the time to move about the house when you're not at home. That is why I asked the cleaner if she could get me a live-in maid, but nobody is willing to stay over. In fact, we are lucky to have the cleaner, because most of the locals are afraid to come here; they believe the Manor is cursed and the curse will also affect them and their families."

"What!" Gerry came to her side and grabbed hold of her arms and began shaking her.

"Hey!" David intervened. "Stop that." He grabbed hold of Gerry pulling him away from Ava who was staring at her husband in fear. "What the hell's wrong with you?"

"We are not moving and that's final. This is my home; you can go but I'm staying," he snarled forcing Ava to face him with a threatening glare.

"Gerry! Gerry!" David shouted noticing the strange look on Gerry's face. "For goodness sake, control yourself."

"Stay out of this!" Gerry yelled, turning to face David. "She wanted to live here as much as I did, so if she doesn't like it, she can bugger off, and you, you can get out of my house right now and take that simpering cow with you."

Ava and David were shocked beyond belief and stared at Gerry as his outburst shook them to the core. The sight of hatred in Gerry's raging, contorted face sent Ava scurrying behind David as he pulled her behind him for protection.

"Go on," Gerry snarled, "and take that miserable bitch with you."

With a threatening gesture, he moved towards David and took a swing at him, but David was faster. He slammed his fist into Gerry's gut, knocking the wind from him, then as he fell forward, David gave him a sharp uppercut and knocked him out cold with one swift blow.

"Oh God, what's wrong with him? Gerry has never acted like this before," Ava cried sinking to her knees beside her unconscious husband.

"Get away from him," David spoke gently as he helped her to her feet. "We don't know what he is capable of doing next. Let me sort this out and you go get a cold, damp cloth from the kitchen that I can put on his head. Woo, wait a minute, who the devil is that?" he gasped when a woman completely covered in black clothing unexpectedly appeared in the doorway.

Ava glanced to where David was staring and felt a cold tremor run through her.

"Gerry and I have seen her before," Ava whispered shakily as she grabbed hold of David's arm. "She is usually standing on the balcony."

Ava felt her throat constrict and was unable to speak, while David felt his jaw drop wide open, when the room temperature unexpectedly dropped and to their horror, the silhouette of a tall man rose out of Gerry's body and drifted away through the corner of the office wall.

"Oh my God," David whispered hoarsely.

"Beware of him! He wants his soul!" the woman warned, pointing to Gerry's prone form, then she too disappeared.

At that precise moment, Gerry groaned and tried to sit up asking what had happened, while Ava and David stood stupefied staring at one another.

"David, Ava," Gerry groaned, "help me up, will you, what am I doing down here?" he said rubbing his stomach. "I feel as if I've been hit with a bloody steam train."

David threw Ava a warning glance not to say anything about what had transpired earlier, and helped Gerry to his feet then sat him down in the chair while Ava poured him a drink and handed it to him.

Gerry threw her a look of gratitude and drank the whiskey down in one straight gulp and sat rubbing his face while David and Ava tried to comprehend the sudden change in Gerry's behaviour.

"Gerry, can you remember anything before you attacked Ava?" David asked.

"What? You must be joking, I would never do anything that would hurt Ava," he snapped angrily. "What the hell are you talking about?"

"I suggested that we move away from here and you suddenly went berserk," Ava said, anxious that Gerry wouldn't react as violently as he had done earlier.

Gerry stared at her in disbelief. "I was going to suggest that myself, by the way, who was that man standing over there by the bookcase?"

David felt his flesh crawl when Gerry indicated towards the far corner of his office where the man had disappeared. Trying hard to keep the situation under control, David asked what the man looked like and how was he dressed.

"To be honest, I couldn't see him very clearly, but what the hell happened for me to attack you, Ava? You know I love you and would never do anything to harm you."

"Gerry," David interrupted, "try to remember what happened in the last few minutes of waking up, it's important that you remember."

"Can I have a coffee? I need to clear my head I feel as if I've been hit with a bulldozer," he grumbled, and ignoring David's questions, he turned towards the door.

"You stay there, Gerry, I'll go put the coffee on," David offered.

"And Ava, you stay here with Gerry, he needs you right now. Can I get you a brandy before I go into the kitchen?" he asked her.

"Yes please, just a small one."

David poured the drink and placed it on the table, and was about to go into the kitchen when he turned asking Gerry if he could remember anything, anything at all. Then felt his voice drain away when seeing another apparition.

"Oh no, not again," he groaned. "Look."

David indicated towards the large oak corner cabinet, from where a ragged child emerged who was rubbing her eyes and crying for her mother.

"I want me mam, please don't hurt me," she cried as she ran stumbling across the centre of the room, then disappeared through the wall opposite.

"What the bloody hell was that all about?" Gerry yelled. Leaping from the chair, he began frantically searching the wall where the child had vanished. "Where did she go?" he cried frantically, as he turned towards David. "We've got to help her."

"You can," they heard a woman saying softly, "you can help us all."

David spun around. "Bloody hell, it's that woman again," he gasped.

The woman who had appeared earlier, lifted the black veil covering her face to reveal the heartbroken features of a woman who had suffered a great loss. Her face that would have once been beautiful, was drawn by lines of suffering, and her beautiful green eyes were filled with tears of sorrow.

"Who do you think she is?" Ava whispered fearfully, clinging to David's arm.

"I don't know, but she looks like you," he said softly with an air of confidence, although he was terrified and shaking inside.

"Beware, he will use you, he will take control of your mind and your body, he wants your soul," she said pointing to Gerry. "It is you he wishes to control, leave before it is too late," she warned before slowly dissolving in an aura of pure white light.

Trembling with fear, the three stared at one another in silence, wondering and worrying what was going to happen next.

Chapter 35
The Homecoming

"Ava, before I go to London, I want you and Sally to go and stay with either your parents or mine."

"But…" Ava began to protest.

"No buts," Gerry was insistent. "I won't listen to another word, and I don't want any arguments not after what happened this morning. I've made up my mind, you and Sally are leaving before I go."

Ava threw David a helpless look appealing for him to intervene, but she knew deep down that what Gerry was suggesting made sense, also David was as much in favour of both she and Sally leaving before they did.

Just then, to Gerry's dismay, a vehicle drew up outside and Sally came racing into the house.

"Mum! Dad!" she called excitedly as she hurried into Gerry's office with a big happy smile on her face. "They've let us all leave school early because the weather forecast says that it will be getting worse and we will be snowed under within the next two days."

The smile died from her face when she noticed the tension within the room.

"What's wrong?" she asked glancing around and seeing the sombre looks on everyone's faces.

Before they could answer, they heard a broad Yorkshire voice calling from the foyer, "I've put your luggage in the entrance, Miss, will there be anything else?"

Ava was the first to find her voice. "Hold on a minute," she called picking up her purse and hurried to the entrance hall to tip the driver. To her surprise after thanking her, he hurried to his vehicle and quickly sped away.

Ava then returned to Gerry's office, where she ushered both Gerry and David into the lounge then went into the kitchen with Sally following close behind questioning what was wrong.

"Sally, darling," Ava began as she filled the kettle, then stopped, wondering how to approach the subject.

"Has Daddy found a way into the attic yet?" Sally asked, her eyes bright and eager.

"No, he hasn't, sweetheart, but he and Uncle David have suggested that we go stay with our family while he is away."

"Oh no," Sally groaned, "I've asked Hilary from school if she wants to stay over and she's accepted. Her father will be dropping her off within the next hour. She's called in at home to say hello to her mum and pick up her nightclothes and some extra warm clothing for when we go outside exploring."

Sally then dropped a bombshell causing Ava to feel a sickening lump rise in her throat. Sally unexpectedly asked if they had a new housekeeper.

"No dear, why do you ask?"

"Oh nothing really, but the lady in the black dress smiled at me when I came in. The bus driver from the college didn't say anything, he just looked at her and said that he would wait by the door. I told him it would be alright for him to come in and get warm but he declined and said he would rather wait at the door."

Meanwhile, Gerry and David were frantically trying to figure out who they could get to stay at the mansion while they were away in London. Gerry knew that it would be a waste of time asking both sets of in-laws to stay after what happened during the night of the party.

"Well, I'm not asking Brenda to bring the children to stay," said David. "My wife's nerves are bad enough as it is if she saw anything untoward, she would have heart failure."

"I understand what you're saying," Gerry replied.

"There is another option though," David suggested hopefully. "There's Alex, what about Alex and his team staying over with Ava and the girls while we're away. He did say that he would come and bring the team if it was alright by you."

Gerry stared at David doubtfully before responding, "I don't think that's such a good idea, even if Ava was willing to agree, I would still be worried sick about Sally and Hilary being alone in the house with a bunch of strangers."

"Come on, Gerry, you know what I am suggesting makes sense. There would be four of them, two women, Don and Alex, and there are plenty of beds for them to sleep in. You know the old saying, there's safety in numbers."

"I don't know; it sounds plausible enough, but I think we should first hear what Ava has to say about the idea." Gerry added reluctantly. "To be honest, we've never met the rest of Alex's team, for all we know they could be a bunch of doped-up hippies."

David could feel his temper rising and was rapidly running out of patience with his friend.

"Bloody hell, Gerry," he snapped, "that's negative thinking; pick up the fucking phone and call him."

Gerry had never seen David so angry, realising that it was himself who was finding excuses not to leave the girls alone with Alex and his team.

He quickly pulled himself together. "I suppose you're right; my nerves are shattered by what's going on here, the sooner we sell this house and get away from it, the better. I'm bound to agree with the local gossip—the bloody place is cursed and haunted."

Chapter 36
The Arrival of Alex and the Team

Gerry glanced at the contact number Alex had given him, he was aware that they were running out of time and there were only ten hours left before the meeting in London, but still he hesitated.

"We don't know him that well and we don't know if the people he works with are to be trusted, I don't know what to do, should I cancel the meeting or not?" Gerry remarked hesitantly.

"For goodness sake, man," David snapped, "you were saying only a few hours ago about how much you trusted him."

"Yes, but that was different, that was his psychic work," Gerry interrupted. "That woman is appearing more often, and I really do believe that she is trying to warn me about something, but what?"

"I understand what you are implying," David snapped, his patience was beginning to wear thin again. "But I think you should leave for your own good, it's you the man is after, not Ava. Sally will be safe with four other people in the house while you're away, so give him a ring now."

Gerry glared at David before reluctantly dialling the number and calling Alex.

"I know this is short notice," he said to Alex. "But could you and your team get here for tomorrow as early as possible?"

"No problem," Alex replied. "We could get there this evening if you wanted, and maybe get some of the cameras set up and be ready for an early morning start."

"The sooner you're here, the better," Gerry responded, "but the problem is that I will be gone for the better part of the week."

"Don't worry about it," Alex commented. "We can stay as long as Ava needs us to, every member of the team is here with me right now. We are already packed and just waiting for you to give the word."

Gerry felt a sense of relief, when knowing that Ava and Sally would be safely taken care of and told Alex that they could come that evening. It would be preferable if they could stay in the Manor with Sally and Hilary, and the rooms would be made ready for their arrival.

David, who was listening, gave him a nod of approval.

"It does say on the news that the weather is going to turn bad by tomorrow morning," Gerry added. "So I suggest that David and I should set off late this afternoon. it's a long run up to London and we don't want to get caught in any accidents and traffic holdups. Not when we have such an important meeting coming up. I'll let Ava know our plans, then she will sleep easy."

Gerry walked over to the open door and turned looking sternly towards David.

"I hope we're doing the right thing," he said, and walked over to the kitchen to inform Ava and Sally of his plans.

Chapter 37
Sad Memories

The Grange felt empty and larger after Gerry and David had left for London. Alex had arrived that evening and had brought along three people—two women and one man—whom he introduced as Helen, Margaret and Brian. They were to accompany him when investigating the Mansion.

Hilary, Sally's school friend, had arrived earlier that day. She had been dropped off by her father who was dubious about her staying at the Grange. He had insisted that, along with being on her best behaviour, if any problems should arise then she should call him immediately and he would come to take her home.

But as soon as she and Sally got their heads together, all thoughts of dos and don'ts dissolved, and the pair raced up the wide staircase and disappeared giggling into Sally's bedroom.

Hearing the girls' constant chatter and giggles, Ava felt an air of despondency and sadness surrounding her. In her mind, she could visualise and hear the sounds of the boy's voices as they used to yell and shout as they cavorted about their rooms in their old home.

Ava was so engrossed in her thoughts that she jumped when Alex approached asking if it would be alright for them to set up the equipment they had brought with them.

"Yes, of course," she replied, hoping he wouldn't notice the tears in her eyes.

"Good," he gave her an reassuring smile. "Are you feeling alright?" he asked when noticing the look of sadness on her face.

"Yes, yes, of course I am, I'm sorry, I was just thinking about the boys, with Gerry and David leaving the house, it makes it feel so empty."

"I understand," he sympathised, "I lost my wife, my mother and my two girls three years ago in a terrorist attack." His voice suddenly filled with emotion and he looked away so she wouldn't notice the pain etched in his face.

"Oh, I'm so sorry, I didn't know," she said, placing a comforting hand on his arm. "Maybe it would help if you shared your sorrow with someone who's had a similar experience."

Alex nodded his head. "I was due to go abroad with my family at the time, and as you can guess as it was our first holiday overseas we were all excited about going. But a big job cropped up and the money was so good that I couldn't refuse the offer. I knew my wife and children were disappointed that I would be staying behind, so as I didn't want to spoil the arrangements we'd made, I asked my mother if she would like to go in my place, of course she jumped at the chance."

Alex was silent and looked away from Ava, then after taking a few deep breaths, he carried on. "Dear God, I can't and will never forgive myself for what happened. They didn't stand a chance, I was told that the girls were splashing about at the water's edge and my wife and mother were lying on the sun loungers, when some foreign bastards shot them dead on the beach. It was a fucking massacre that day and not one of the armed guards lifted a finger to protect them. You know what, they aren't supposed to kill one another; it's supposed to be against their religious belief."

"Well, why do the tourist operators encourage people to holiday in those countries?" Ava asked in astonishment.

"Money, greed, that's what it's all about," Alex sneered, "money, big money."

For a few moments, Ava thought that Alex was going to break down but he managed to regain control of himself. However, the bitter memories of what had happened to his family would never be forgotten nor forgiven.

"Come on," he added as cheerfully as he could, "let's put the sad memories behind us, we can't change what was meant to be, can we?"

Ava couldn't help but admire his courage at the devastation wreaked on him and his family.

"No," she replied shaking her head, "would you mind me asking how long ago?"

"Three years, the girls were only four," he said bitterly.

"I'm sorry, I shouldn't have asked," Ava responded.

"It's alright, I shouldn't have sworn like that."

"I wouldn't worry too much about it," she said with a forced laugh, "Gerry and David use it all the time. To be honest, I was always concerned about the boys picking up on their bad language."

Ava's voice tapered off when she felt herself shaking with sobs as the distressing memories flooded through her.

"Come on," he said, placing an arm around her heaving shoulders and leading her to a chair. "It's something you will never forget but in time, the pain will ease and you will come to terms with what has happened."

"I hope you are right," she said tearfully wiping her nose with her handkerchief. "I'm sorry."

"Don't be; it can happen to anybody nowadays, and the criminals always get away unpunished."

Chapter 38
The Attic

As soon as the cameras and electrical equipment had been placed in each of the downstairs rooms and switched on, masses of plasmatic orbs could be seen darting in every direction of the rooms they had been set.

Ava watched in fascination as the orbs swirled around them, then gasped when seeing the blurred figure of a tall man float across the room then disappear through the far wall.

Within minutes, every camera was catching hazy indistinct images moving along the corridors and rooms.

"Why aren't they focused more clearly?" Ava whispered to Helen.

"I can't say for certain," Helen replied, "but they do need a large amount of electrical energy to make themselves visible, and there is a huge amount of spirit moving about here. If it was just one or two, then maybe we would be able to make out who they are, but as there are so many showing themselves at once, there's no chance of us getting a clear image."

Just then Alex spotted the figure of a woman who was moving up the staircase.

"Quick, somebody get the camcorder and get onto the staircase, there's a woman going up there."

"Did you see what she was wearing?" Ava asked breathless, and excited at the same time.

Then she let out a startled cry when she realised the girls were in the upstairs bedroom.

"Oh no, the girls are upstairs, please don't let them see her," she cried.

Alex took hold of her hand. "Come on, don't worry about it," he said, pulling her behind him. "I don't believe she was heading for Sally's room. I think she was going to the attic."

Ava threw him a worried glance. "I hope you're right," she whispered.

"She is different from the other apparitions we've been seeing," he added.

"What do you mean, different?" Ava asked, stumbling along behind him.

"This one is young, blonde and beautiful. Her hair is curled with ringlets and she is wearing a long white wedding dress. She seems to know where she is heading, so I'm going to follow her and find out where that is."

"Please be careful," Ava whispered.

"I will."

Just then, Brian caught up to Alex with the camcorder and passed it to him. Alex then raced along the balcony with Ava and Brian following close behind until reaching the dimly lit attic staircase. He ground to a sudden halt when seeing the young woman about to enter the attic. At the same time, she was being greeted by an older woman of identical features who could have been her mother.

The lady was wearing a long blue, silk gown, and the sleeves of her gown were decorated with delicate pale grey lace cuffs. Her hair was as red as the flames in a fire, and when her green eyes met Alex's, he felt a strange shudder of recognition run through him when realising that the older woman was identical to Ava.

The two women joined hands, stopped and turned to face Alex, before the older woman beckoned to Alex with her free hand, turned and disappeared through the locked attic door.

At first, he was stunned by what he was seeing, then shouted "Follow me" as he bounded up the staircase. "We've got to get in there."

Ava followed him until reaching the last few steps, Alex stood and fidgeted with a gadget he had taken from his pocket and placed it into the first lock.

To their surprise, they heard a ping and the lock snapped open. Then, with trembling hands, he tried the second lock; this also snapped open. For a few seconds, they looked at one another unsure of what to do.

"Well, in for a penny," he said warily.

"In for a pound," Ava finished for him.

Carefully, Alex pushed open the creaking door not knowing what to expect as he cautiously peered inside.

"Phew," he muttered, turning towards Ava and gasping for air. "It's obvious this place hasn't been opened in years." He stood for a few moments, allowing the smell of decay and some other unpleasant odour that he didn't recognise to evaporate before he entered the attic.

At first glance, all he could see was a mass of cobwebs and a deep coating of dust, and what appeared to be large amounts of old junk stacked in the doorway. As there were no windows or electricity in the attic, he was unable to see any further than the dull light that was emanating from the dimly lit staircase.

"I'd better go get a torch," he murmured softly as he peered into the darkness. "You wait here."

"Not likely," Ava announced loudly, "you're not leaving me on my own up here."

"Come on then." Alex made his way past her, then taking her by the arm, he carefully led Ava down the creaking uncarpeted staircase until reaching the hall.

"There are some old paraffin lamps in the cellar, and paraffin," Ava suggested.

"No, we have camping lamps in the cars, I'll go get them; they're battery-operated." He stood thinking for a few moments. "I would guess that we will be needing about four for that space upstairs."

Alex left Ava waiting with Brian until he had returned with the lamps. "You stay here, Brian, with the cameras. Ava! You come with me upstairs," he said in a voice filled with excitement. "I'll go first."

With Alex leading the way, Ava felt a surge of confidence that they were about to discover what was in the attic. They went along the balcony without any problems and up the dimly lit staircase where Alex stopped to switch on the four lamps.

Breathless with excitement, he said, "You take two and I'll the other two, and here we go." Alex stepped forward into the massive cluttered open space. "We are about to make history," he said. Then uttered a loud ouch when he banged his head on the low rafters. "Hell, it's bigger than I expected, and it stinks!" he exclaimed as he made his way through the dusty relics. "I need more light over here," he called.

Holding the lamp as high as she could, Ava edged her way steadily forward towards Alex, at the same time being careful not to stand or trip over any of the objects that lay strewn about the floor.

"The attic must have been used in the past," Alex said turning towards Ava and hanging one of the lanterns on a hook that was screwed into the old oak beam. "Or there wouldn't have been these hooks fitted in the ceiling for lights, and if my guess is correct, when you look at the house from the outside there is a round window where the attic is situated, and that window would have been somewhere in the centre of that wall over there."

Alex pointed into the darkest recess of the attic.

"Therefore, the window has been boarded up, that is why it is so dark in here."

Feeling pleased with himself at his hypothesis, Alex turned his attention back to where he was heading and before long he had found another hook in the ceiling.

"Ava, can you bring another lamp over here?" Alex indicated for Ava to come closer.

But at that moment, a number of piercing screams echoed from Sally's bedroom followed by thunderous sounds and banging from below.

"My God, what's happening?" Ava shouted as the whole area began vibrating and the temperature dropped to freezing.

"We must have upset something, come on," he yelled grabbing her arm and dragging her out of the attic. They raced down the staircase towards Sally's bedroom where they found Hilary hysterical and screaming.

"What happened?" Ava asked Sally as she attempted to calm the screaming child.

"There was a man standing in the room, and he walked through the wall over there," Sally replied in a calm, unruffled monotone.

Ava looked at her, puzzled, while Alex escorted the shaking girl downstairs who was crying for her father and wanted to go home.

Meanwhile, Ava brought Sally down stairs and seated her in the lounge, but when she looked into Gerry's office, she gave a cry of alarm seeing that everything was in a shambles.

Furniture, books, all of Gerry's paperwork, computer, printer, shredder, etc. was strewn about his office, along with the equipment that Alex's team had set up. Helen, Margaret and Brian were cowering behind the sofa that was upturned in the far corner of the room.

Stunned by the sight of the carnage, Ava reached for the phone and called Hilary's father, asking for him to come and pick up his daughter right away.

He wanted to know what was wrong and Ava said that she would explain everything when he arrived. All Ava wanted to do was to get the hysterical child away from the house, and she was pleased that Alex had managed to calm her before her father arrived.

In the meantime, Helen, Margaret and Brian were salvaging the damaged equipment and packing it away.

"I'm sorry, Alex, but we're leaving. This thing is far too big for us to cope with, we know when to call it quits," Brian said, glancing fearfully about the room. "I'll leave your equipment but we're taking ours, I'm sorry but that's how it stands." Brian went to help the other two to salvage their equipment, and once it was packed, they left.

"Are you leaving as well?" Ava asked apprehensively. "If so, can we come with you?"

Alex stood thoughtfully for a few moments before making his decision. "No, I'm staying. I want to know what's in the attic; someone doesn't want us to find out what it is."

Sally broke away from her mother's hand. "I'm going back to my room," she said skipping along the hall and bounding up the staircase.

"What? No," Ava shrieked, and was about to chase after her when Alex grabbed hold of her arm.

"Wait," he whispered, "let her go, didn't you notice how unperturbed she was when all of this was occurring. I believe your daughter is the catalyst; she is being used by whatever is the main power here. And I believe that power is the man that Hilary saw."

"Oh no, not Sally."

"Yes, Sally."

"Oh dear Lord, protect her," Ava whispered in a strangled tone. "If that is so, then more's the reason why I should be with my daughter."

"No, let her go, no harm will come to her. We must get back to the attic immediately."

At first, Ava hesitated then reluctantly did as Alex asked and accompanied him back up the stairs and into the attic.

"I'll light the last two lamps now then we can move forward and hang them as we go."

"Wait," Ava whispered, "that trunk is open, it wasn't open earlier when we first came into the attic."

"You're right, somebody must want us to see what's in there."

Alex moved over to the trunk. "Look," he pointed to a scrap of paper that had been torn from the old diary lying at the bottom of the trunk. "There's some writing on it, it looks like a letter." Alex picked up the paper and began reading then stopped, shaking his head in disbelief.

"Ava," he gasped, "you are not going to believe this; her father, her own bloody father." As Alex handed her the letter, she was surprised to see tears coursing down his cheeks.

"Sit down," he said gently. "Over here beside me." He motioned to the box where he was seated.

Ava strode over the items scattered about the floor and seated herself beside Alex and began reading the faded handwriting.

"Oh good gracious," she gasped, staring at Alex when she had finished reading of the horrendous torture crudely forced upon the young woman.

"This is from the diary of Elizabeth Goldberg the girl who was…"

Ava stared horrified at the letter she had just read.

"What can we do?" she asked.

"It's too late now, there's nothing we can do but hand the letter over to the right people."

"But they will know we have been in the attic!" she cried.

"Shit, I didn't think of that."

"There must be something..." Her voice suddenly trailed off into a whisper when she saw the apparitions of two women appear, and both were smiling.

For a few moments, both Ava and Alex couldn't move, transfixed by what they were seeing.

"Alex, look," Ava said, keeping her voice low. "They are moving across the attic towards the far wall. It's too dark I can't make out where they are going but I think they want us to follow."

They watched as the figures slowly disappeared into the dark recess of the attic.

"What do you think we should do?" Ava's voice trembled as she spoke.

"I'm not quite certain, but I think they are trying to show us something," he replied. Alex picked up the lamp and moved forward with Ava clinging to his free arm.

"Are you alright to keep going?" he asked when noticing that she was trembling.

"Yes, so long as we stay close."

"It looks like a bed over in that far corner," he said, stopping to hang the lantern onto the lowest beam, and staring into the dancing shadows. "Oh my God," he muttered softly, turning to Ava.

Ava felt herself sway when seeing the mummified body of a woman dressed in discoloured, ragged wedding attire laid on the bed.

At the precise moment, the beautiful young woman appeared dressed in a white wedding gown, and alongside her was her was the woman dressed in a pale blue silk gown.

The white silk, lace wedding dress neckline was modestly square, with a tight-fitting bodice, puffed sleeves to the elbow and fitted to the wrists with small pearl buttons. The lower skirt of the dress fell in three tiers of silken lace and each tier was embroidered with lace frill. Her veil and train was held in place with a sparkling diamond tiara. The train was interwoven with pearls and tiny blue and pink floral Forget-Me-Knot. On the third finger of her left hand that she held out towards them was a beautiful ring. This was a large white pearl surrounded by diamonds and on either side were two larger diamonds. On her feet, she wore white satin shoes.

The older woman wore a splendid gown of pale blue silk that ruffled around her neck; the bodice was tight fitting and the sleeves came to her elbows; the skirt fell to just above ankle length where they could see she was wearing pale blue satin shoes. Her hands and arms were covered with pale blue lace gloves, and she was also wearing a diamond tiara. In an instant, Ava and Alex realised who they were.

Without any feeling of fear, Alex asked, "Are you Hannah and Elizabeth?"

The older woman smiled as she replied, "Yes we are."

"Do you want your daughter to have a Christian burial?" Ava asked hesitantly. "Or do you want her remains to stay sealed in this attic?"

"No, she stays here," a male voice unexpectedly thundered. "She was born, lived and died here, and this is where she will stay."

Hannah suddenly appeared dressed in mourning black.

"Give my daughter a Christian burial, and place her in my own family's tomb," she said in an authoritative tone. "Do not listen to him; he is evil; he murdered my daughter."

A look of pure hatred flashed across Lord Goldberg's face. "You will be sorry you ever entered here," he snarled, glaring into Ava and Alex's eyes.

Ava shrank in fear and scuttled behind Alex, who firmly stood his ground.

"We will do as you say, ma'am," Alex attested firmly. "We will make sure that she is buried in your family burial ground."

Goldberg's face twisted with rage. "You will all be sorry!" he roared as he slowly evaporated into the shadows of the darkness, shouting and screaming profanities.

"Thank you," Hannah acknowledged, drawing the veil back from her face where they saw that the anguished features had now disappeared. In their place was the beauty that had once charmed many admirers. She had regained her stunning qualities as the lines of sorrow and despair were gone and wiped away from her beautiful face.

No longer was she dressed in mourning attire, but in the beautiful blue silk gown that she would have been wearing at her daughter's wedding.

Hannah then acknowledged what Alex and Ava had done; they had released her and her daughter from the perpetual punishment that her husband had brought upon them.

Both Elizabeth and Hannah gazed at them for a short while longer, then after giving Ava and Alex a smile of gratitude, they slowly disappeared within a beautiful silver halo of light.

"What do we do now?" Ava whispered, shivering from fright at the thought of the man returning.

"The first thing we do is get downstairs and call the police and tell them what we've found. Then after they've been, we get the hell out of here."

Ava couldn't agree more. After giving a last sorrowful look at the mummified corpse on the makeshift bed, they left the attic.

Both were glancing fearfully about them and clung to one another as they crossed the landing, half expecting the dreaded Lord Goldberg to appear at any minute.

Then, as they neared Sally's room, Ava opened the door slightly and peeped inside, where to her surprise she saw that her daughter was oblivious to what had occurred. She was hard at work studying for her latest exams.

"Leave her," Alex whispered in a soft tone, "she won't come to any harm, not after what's just happened."

Ava felt uncertain, but after feeling Alex's hand of support on her arm, she quietly pulled the door to, but left it slightly ajar so that they could hear if Sally needed them. She headed down the staircase with Alex into the lounge.

"I think we should have some coffee," Alex said moving towards the kitchen. "It will help calm our nerves. Afterwards, we can call the police and explain what we have found in the attic."

Ava agreed.

Chapter 39
Death at the Grange

Just as Ava was about to call Gerry, Alex asked if she had ever been into the cellar as Gerry had mentioned that she was afraid to go down into it. Ava explained that she had avoided going down into the cellar because she was afraid of mice, plus it was also very cold down there. She didn't say anything about the eerie sensations of someone walking behind her nor the heavy breathing she heard when reaching the bottom of the stone steps and entering the cellar.

Gerry had explored the entire area below when they had first viewed the property and was surprised by the immensity of the space that he found, but didn't say any more.

"Do you mind if I took a look around down there while were waiting for the police?" Alex asked.

"No," Ava replied, "there are lights down there, so take your time. Oh and be careful of the handrail, it's loose. Gerry keeps saying he will fix it but he never has done. So you go ahead. I'll wait here for the police."

Alex picked up his camcorder, inserted fresh batteries and went off to the cellar while Ava waited impatiently for the police to arrive.

Due to the extreme weather conditions, it took the police an hour to arrive at the Grange. First to arrive were four police cars, followed by an incident vehicle, then the medical examiner who arrived last in a dark windowed SUV.

Upon their arrival, Ava led them upstairs to the attic where the mummified body lay and left them to carry out their investigation.

She gave strict instructions for them not to disturb her daughter who was in her room studying for her exams. Then she returned to her office and attempted to concentrate on completing the features for the magazine.

Meanwhile, Alex was investigating the farthest wall in the cellar where he had noticed a difference in the colouring of the cement sealing the stone wall. He presumed that this was the location where the builder had sealed the opening after the Hall had collapsed into the cellar.

Alex stood back but as he began filming the sealed aperture, he gasped when seeing the hazy figure of a man with a huge dog by his side beginning to emerge through the stone wall.

At first, Alex was overwhelmed by catching the apparition and phenomena on film, but when the man had completely emerged and materialised, he stood and stared at Alex, who felt himself cringing under the man's steady hard glare that was full of venomous hatred.

Alex noted that the man stood well over six feet tall, was handsome with piercing black eyes, and appeared to be around his late forties to early fifties.

His long black hair was tied behind his neck with a leather thong. Alex could only guess that the clothing he wore was from the eighteenth century. His long scarlet jacket covered a highly decorated long silk waistcoat with a lace cravat around his neck. The breeches matching his jacket came to just below his knees, and the long white stockings were tucked beneath the breeches.

On his feet were deep red buckled shoes, and he carried a riding whip in one hand and a tall scarlet hat in the other. His hands were covered by red leather gloves.

Alex lowered his camcorder and faced the apparition, before the man turned and retreated with the dog through the wall.

Alex watched, completely bewildered, yet overjoyed by the experience, before realising that he had seen that face before, and remembered that it was in a portrait in a museum in Harrogate.

My God, he muttered to himself, *it's Samuel Goldberg. If he didn't die out there on the moors, then somebody must have killed him and buried him down here in the cellar of the old Hall.*

The mere thought sent a shudder racing through him. Then as soon as the probability came to him, the echoing sound of rapacious laughter reverberated around the cavernous cellar.

Alex covered his ears to block out the deafening racket and spun around to see from what direction the loathsome sound was coming. But it was too late, in the semi darkness he did not see the three-pronged hay-fork being lifted by unseen hands come his way to be thrust deep inside his chest.

Meanwhile, Ava was busy keeping out of the way while the police carried out their work upstairs. She was pleased when they left, some hours later, taking the mummified remains and other articles with them, leaving two officers Jones, and Wilks, guarding the entrance hall down stairs.

Sally however, had been very quiet throughout the whole incident and had stayed in her room, which Ava thought was a little unusual.

Sally, as a rule, was an inquisitive child who enjoyed being involved in whatever was occurring, So Ava decided to go up to her room to see if she was alright.

Ava was still nervous about the previous encounter and walked towards the staircase constantly glancing about herself to ensure no-one else was there. She ascended the stairs and walked along the balcony until coming to Sally's room, where she stopped and tapped gently on the door before entering and peeping around the door.

Ava smiled when she saw that Sally was fast asleep at her desk and went over to wake her, but when she touched her shoulder, Ava felt that it was cold and stiff.

"No!" she screamed, "No!" Ava touched her again, but this time Sally dropped to the floor and lay motionless and rigid, staring up at the ceiling through vacant glazed eyes.

"Sally! Sally!" Ava screamed.

Dropping to her knees, she lifted her daughter and cradled her in her arms.

"No Sally! You can't die! I won't let you!" she cried, rocking backwards and forwards clutching the dead girl closely to her chest.

Alerted by the screams, the two officers looked at one another, then raced through the hall and up the staircase to Sally's room, where they found Ava on the floor still cradling Sally.

"Oh shit!" PC Jones whispered, PC Wilks took one look at the distraught woman and dropped to his knees by her side, then gently relaxed her grip on the dead girl and helped her to her feet.

Despite her protests, he led her out of the room while PC Jones began CPR in the hope of restarting Sally's breathing.

From the first moment of seeing Sally's limp body, it was obvious that the child was dead and nothing could be done to resuscitate her.

Nevertheless, PC Jones did all he could before finally admitting defeat. He gently lay her body flat on the carpeted floor, crossed her arms over her chest, then covered her with the duvet from her bed.

By this time, the ambulance had arrived and after the doctor had carried out a thorough examination, he declared Sally dead.

The autopsy was to show that she had died from an embolism to the brain. It was a delayed action that could have occurred at any time and was believed to have been caused by the fatal car accident that had killed her two brothers and Aunt Caroline.

Chapter 40
Epilogue

The car carrying Sergeant Watson and Officer Drake stopped on the drive just a short distance away from the mansion's main front entrance.

"How the hell do we tell a man that his daughter is dead from a brain embolism and his wife has hung herself? And not only that, but we've found a corpse in the cellar with a hayfork stuck in him?" Watson said, turning to face Drake.

"I don't rightly know, sir," Drake replied, "but I'm sure you will find the right words."

"Huh," he grunted. "Well, Mr Wilson should be home any time now," he mumbled, looking at his watch and began rehearsing in his mind how he was going to explain the sudden, unexpected deaths.

Sergeant Watson hated being the bearer of bad news, especially where children were involved, but somebody had to do it.

He had tried ringing Gerry Wilson's mobile phone, but all he'd received was static. It was the same with the main police station; he couldn't get through to anybody.

Just then a car drew up and a dishevelled man with a briefcase clambered wearily out and went towards the door.

"Excuse me sir, are you Mr Gerry Wilson?" Watson called as he got out of the car with Drake and moved towards Gerry.

The man turned and stared at him with a blank expression on his face. "Yes, I am! Why do you ask?"

"Sir, I have some rather, unpleasant news for you," Watson said hesitantly. "Could we go inside where we can talk."

"Yes, come inside where it's warmer. My wife is expecting me and she has put some coffee on," he said smiling at the two officers, who passed a puzzled look between one another.

At that moment, Superintendent Banks arrived and called to them from his car.

"I've been trying to reach you for the past half hour but all I got was static down the phone. I'm afraid you've had a wasted journey."

"What do you mean?" Watson asked, slithering on the icy snow as he moved towards the vehicle's open window.

"Mr Wilson and his business partner were killed in a pile-up on the M1 motorway half an hour ago. There were no survivors."

Back Page

Who haunts Goldberg Hall? Could it be the past owners? Or did someone from the more recent times meet a cruel fate there?

Could it be the woman and child, who Ava saw walking along the road towards Waterfall River?

Or Jack Armstrong the builder, who renovated the Hall and gave it a new name—The Grange? He was discovered frozen to death in a solid block of ice inside his car.

There is a strong possibility that it could be Lord Goldberg himself who raped his own daughter and died from a revenge killing.

There are many theories as to whom, or what, haunts The Manor; nevertheless, the locals stay away from Gallows Hill where the old Hall used to stand. They know the rumours of the hanging Goldberg judges. The remaining part of the Hall has now been refurbished and sold to a young couple with three children.

Unknown to the new owners is the fact that not everyone leaves the Hall alive.

Perhaps the only people who could explain the inexplicable happenings there are the dead souls themselves who haunt Goldberg Hall.

Elisa Wilkinson

Ingram Content Group UK Ltd.
Milton Keynes UK
UKHW052030090423
419773UK00019B/1029

9 781398 477650